Seasons of Aromatherapy

Seasons
of
Aromatherapy

Hundreds of *Restorative Recipes*
and *Sensory Suggestions*

PAULA M. BOUSQUET & JUDITH FITZSIMMONS

CONARI PRESS
Berkeley, California

Printed in the United States of America on recycled paper.
Conari Press books are distributed by Publishers Group West.

Cover design and illustration by Martha Newton Furman
Botanical illustrations by Martha Newton Furman
Book design by Claudia Smelser

Library of Congress Cataloging-in-Publication Data

Bousquet, Paula M.
    Seasons of aromatherapy ; hundreds of restorative recipes and sensory
suggestions / Paula M. Bousquet & Judith Fitzsimmons.
        p.   cm.
    Includes index.
    ISBN: 1–57324–144–x (hbk.)
    1. Aromatherapy. I. Fitzsimmons, Judith. II. Title.
RM666.A68B68   1998   98–45991
615'.321—dc21   CIP

Our thanks to New World Library for allowing us to use a recipe excerpted from the *Complete Book of Essential Oils and Aromatherapy* by Valerie Ann Worwood, copyright © 1991. Reprinted with permission of New World Library, Novato, CA 94949.

    98 99 00 01 RRD(C) 1 2 3 4 5 6 7 8 9 10

DISCLAIMER

This book was designed and written to provide information about and methods of use of the subject matter covered. This information is not intended to be used to treat, diagnose, or prescribe, and is in no way to be considered as a substitute for consultation with a duly licensed health care professional.

Dedicated to Brian, bright star rising.

—Paula M. Bousquet

My thanks to Mom for the desire, to Chelsea for the inspiration, and to Mark for his everlasting patience and support.

—Judith Fitzsimmons

Seasons of Aromatherapy

FOREWORD

Several evenings ago, the harvest moon was full and
rising up and over the buildings. It was a glorious sight and
preceding it, leading it, was a bright star. I watched the star
leading the full moon, and the full moon racing after the star
across the great bow of the sky for most of the evening. It
was beautiful, a simple pleasure that felt warm and happy.

There are books like that, too, that give you a feeling of
deep satisfaction and simple pleasure in the reading. A book
that is beautifully designed, full of information, practical, and
calming is a joy to read.

Seasons of Aromatherapy is just such a book. When I
opened it, I read it immediately and felt calm inside as I
raced through the pages. I made a cup of tea to slow down
and savor the words. I took the manuscript outside to read it
under the arbor of the Alchemist Rose. I walked with it
down my curved garden path, brushing against the Lemon
Verbena tree that scents the air with its lemon-like essence,
and I read about Lemon. I enjoyed reading new recipes for
one of my favorite essential oils and took pleasure in the
quotations that accompany the text.

This book is an excellent guide for anyone new to aromatherapy and to the joys of using essential oils for therapy and indulgence. The recipes are logical, easy to follow, and a delight to use. Even aromatherapy novices will not be intimidated and will instantly be able to compose bath blends, house sprays, massage oils, and health remedies.

Seasons of Aromatherapy engages the beginner like a friend holding your hand. It will effortlessly transport you into the uses and joys of essential oils. This lovely book is the perfect first step in your quest for aromatic knowledge. It wisely limits the essential oils to the twelve most useful and offers hundreds of practical applications: historical uses, special home and gift uses, and everyday uses for child, pet, and home care, plus therapeutic uses for colds and flus. They range from restorative recipes to sensual suggestions to sleep potions.

Aromas entice and exhilarate, educate and heal. *Seasons of Aromatherapy* will enlighten those who are new to the art and science of aromatherapy and will charm those of us who have been involved with this art for a longer time.

Aromatherapy is big news now and growing at an exponential rate, and books that provide responsible education and endless pleasure are needed more than ever.

Seasons of Aromatherapy is a welcome addition to the aromatic literature—for newcomers as well as devoted followers of the art.

Jeanne Rose
September 1998
San Francisco, California

To smell green things continuously will keep anyone in perfect health.

—*Anacreon*

The

Essentials

of

Aromatherapy

*I*F YOU PICKED UP THIS BOOK, you've probably heard something about aromatherapy and want to learn a bit more about it. Congratulations! Welcome to a world where you can address a variety of ailments and beauty concerns in a natural, healthful way. In addition, you'll enjoy the physical and emotional benefits of this healing method, which has been used for centuries.

If you've used Vicks VapoRub™ for cold-caused congestion, liniment for muscle strains, or Noxema™ to cleanse your skin, you have already been using aromatherapy, and you didn't even know it!

There are many full-featured, encyclopedia-type books on aromatherapy. These books are available at the library or on your bookstore's shelves. These books are wonderful references, interestingly written, and well researched.

The approach we took with this book is different. This book is designed as a recipe book, a letter to a friend, a dabble into aromatherapy. Just imagine sitting with us, having a nice cup of tea, and discussing the many ways in which we use aromatherapy.

Whether you are skeptical about aromatherapy, as so many of our friends were, or open-minded about it, this book will help you incorporate aromatherapy into your everyday life. Based on the months and seasons of the year, *Seasons of Aromatherapy* provides information in a chatty, *"why not try it out now?"* sort of way.

As you know, each season has its own challenges: summer's sunburn, bug bites, poison ivy, and gardening aches; winter's colds, depression, gift-giving, and parties. *Seasons of Aromatherapy* approaches all these challenges with pleasing, aromatic suggestions. This book also covers the seasons of the individual, the cyclical patterns of women, and the beauty and health concerns of everyone in your family.

While there are over 150 oils readily available in the marketplace, we've limited the number of oils used through most of this book to twelve—the twelve we consider essential. We've been cost-conscious—as we think you are—and we've presented practical, everyday uses of aromatherapy in the context of step-by-step directions, recipes, hints, and tips for each season, month, night, and day. In addition, we've added twelve "bonus" oils, one for each month, especially for *you*. These oils are great for pampering and self-indulgence, things we all can use more of.

We hope this book piques your interest, entertains you, and gives you concrete ways to enhance your life with aromatherapy. If you care about your home, saving money, and creating things of beauty, this book is for you.

When you incorporate aromatherapy into your surroundings, you'll find them more clean, scented, and calming. You may not know exactly what is different about your life, but you'll *feel* the difference right away. Enjoy!

Essentially yours,
—*Paula and Judi*

About This Book

There are twelve chapters in this book. Each chapter features a month and a specific essential oil. The oil of the month is highlighted in the recipes for that month. Throughout the book, we discuss aromatherapy as it relates to beauty, children, health, home, personal care, and pets.

So start wherever you want or wherever you are in the calendar. If you doubted that you would ever find a foot spray that could prevent your teenager's sneakers from walking out of the house on their own, or a remedy for fatigue, see the index for an alphabetical list of all the recipes. If, on the other hand, you always find February a difficult month to handle because you have to fight off the post-holiday blues, the frostbite that is threatening your toes, and the fact that again this year, you are not going to be swept off your feet by the Valentine's Day knight in shining armor, then wait no longer, go directly (do not pass Go) to February.

WHY ARE WE DOING THIS?

After I picked up my aromatherapy "starter kit" book and eight oils at the bookstore in which I was working for the holiday season, I started dabbling with the oils. They were fun, and I got interesting results. The first time Judi found out about them was when she walked into my house and asked me what I did to make the place feel so cozy.

Once she was interested, Judi wanted to know how to make blends like I did. Because many of my blends were "off the cuff," using what smelled good together or went well logically, it was difficult for me to tell her how to make them. She made me start measuring and writing down what I was doing and making so she could recreate my results at her house.

Telling someone how to recreate a recipe made me start thinking about aromatherapy in a new way. It was not only for my personal fun and aesthetic reward, but other people could use my ideas to make themselves and their homes feel better, too.

—Paula

I remember when I went to Paula's house; I was a first-time mom and was feeling a bit overwhelmed. I walked into her house and it felt more warm and inviting. That's when she told me about aromatherapy, and how she was using it not only for its emotional impact but for skin and hair care as well. I remember thinking, "There must be something to this stuff," and that's when I began my own exploration into the world of essential oils.

My focus is my daughter. I want to give her the best and most natural of treatments. From teething pain and diaper rash to bathing, shampooing, and moisturizing those tender little cheeks, Chelsea continues to be a wonderful recipient of the terrific medicinal and aesthetic benefits of aromatherapy.

Now I can't start a day without my regime of essential oil usage. I may go out without my makeup on, but it is a very rare day that doesn't start with aromatherapy.

—Judi

WHAT IS AROMATHERAPY?

Aromatherapy is the use of aromatic plant essences to bring about positive changes in health, both in mind and body. It's all-natural, holistic (in the sense of being one with the earth), nontoxic, safe for children and pets, efficient, effective, thrifty, and beautiful. Aromatherapy can enhance your appearance, your home, your children, and your life.

One of the oldest proven methods of healing, aromatherapy has been used successfully for centuries. In recent years, its popularity has been revived due to people's willingness to improve their mental, emotional, and physical well-being in a more natural and pure manner.

If you're still not convinced, just look around you. Aromatherapy is already in many products you know and use. Cough drops, mouthwash, chewing gum, hair spray, furniture oils, cleansers, mothballs, perfumes, herbal teas, and citronella candles, to name just a few, all use the essences of aromatherapy, usually indicated by "natural flavorings" or "flavor" on the label.

A frequently made assumption about aromatherapy is that it is simply the smell that has an effect. The real beauty of aromatherapy is that the essences work on a cellular and physical level, and also in the emotional, intellectual, spiritual, and aesthetic areas of your life.

Now that you've gotten over the impression that aromatherapy is a mysterious hobby used in the basement only by people who are always doing something weird, let's make you even more comfortable about working with aromatherapy.

THE LANGUAGE OF AROMATHERAPY

We've already used the term *essence,* which describes the concentrated oil of various flowers, fruits, herbs, and plants. While the use of these essences is called *aromatherapy,* each individual oil is often called an *essential oil.* Modern scientific research has proven that essential oils are potent, with remarkable medicinal properties.

Many aromatherapists call the combination of oils for a specific purpose *blending* or *preparing a recipe,* or even *creating a potion.* To keep you from wondering if we are standing over a caldron in the dark of night with a black cat (although one of us does own a black cat), and candles burning eerily, we refer to the process as *preparing a recipe* to create a *blend.* But if you are telling your mother-in-law about this, go ahead, say *potion,* just to reinforce her lament that you were never good enough for her child.

You can call them blends, potions, or recipes; it depends on your mood. If you are feeling mystical and esoteric when creating, call them potions. If you are feeling spiritual and balanced, call them blends. If you are feeling pragmatic and practical, call them recipes. Any way you look at it, these oils provide centuries-old solutions to physical, mental, and emotional conditions in a natural way.

IT MAKES SENSE,
IT SAVES MONEY, SO WHY NOT?

If you're not convinced, look at it this way: this stuff makes sense—financially, organically, and beautifully. Chances are your budget is straining from the extraneous expense of room deodorizers, mouth deodorizers, laundry deodorizers, clothing deodorizers, and pet deodorizers—until you are deodorized right into a fiscal frenzy.

Even if you buy the store brand of mouthwash, you still pay (taking into account sale prices and coupons) a minimum of a dollar a bottle. For 15¢, you can mix up to nine drops of peppermint essential oil into a quart of water and get the same results. Not only does peppermint smell and taste good, but it is also an antiseptic. And those fussy (or discriminating) people, who we all know and love, can tailor the recipe to meet their most discerning taste. If you don't like peppermint mouthwash, try a combination of eucalyptus and fennel for an exciting morning mouth experience.

Essential oils are concentrated, so you only have to use a little bit. With a small inventory of oils, you can create a multitude of solutions to your everyday concerns. We are suggesting twelve basic oils that you can combine in an unlimited number of ways to create all the blends in this book, and other blends that you will discover to solve unique concerns.

Aromatherapy can also appeal to your ecological soul. Essential oils work in harmony with the earth. They come from the earth, and when you use them, are organically re-absorbed, thus returning harmlessly what has been taken.

Just another point: the oils come in small, dark glass bottles. Since you use just a few drops per recipe, they last a long time. You can also clean the bottles and reuse them to hold your custom blends, or you can recycle the glass.

METHODS OF USE

There are several ways to use the blends you create: water-based, oil-based, or just straight essences.

The water-based uses, such as in baths, whirlpools, saunas, showers, and room sprays, are created by mixing the suggested oil(s) into a designated amount of water. Even with the miracle of aromatherapy, oil and water still don't mix, so you must shake (or stir) these blends before each use.

Oil-based blends are massaged into some part of the body. Lower-back pain, headaches, and common colds, for example, can be helped by oil-based blends.

Here is a quick reference when creating your own blends:

METHOD OF USE	NUMBER OF DROPS
Bath	3–5 drops into the water
Undiluted for the scent	1 drop on each of your favorite spots
Soap	20 drops per 4 ounces of liquid soap

Massage	15 drops per ounce of oil
Loofah	1 drop on loofah
Shampoo/Conditioner	3 drops per ounce
Face Cream	6–8 drops per ounce of cream
Mist	10 drops per quart of distilled water
Compress	5 drops in a small bowl of water
More Hair Care	3 drops oil rubbed on brush bristles

Armed with facts about essential oils and their characteristics, you can let your imagination run free as you create blends to fit your every mood and need. There are also some reat commercial products that augment the use of aromatherapy, including:

- ⊷ diffusers
- ⊷ lamp rings
- ⊷ pendants
- ⊷ beads

But don't forget to have fun and experiment with your own ideas:

- ⊷ air sprays, potpourri, sachets
- ⊷ great gift ideas, including scented handkerchiefs, ornaments, book marks, candles

❧ I'm one of those people who doesn't want the hassles associated with filling out order forms, adding the appropriate sales tax, and then waiting four to six weeks for whatever it is that I have forgotten I ordered. On the other hand, I am equally concerned about getting the most bang for my buck.

And as Paula just said to me (yes, she's leaning over my shoulder as I type), "You're probably going to talk about establishing a relationship with your local health food store owner." Well, she's right. That's exactly what I did. My health store owner offers me a retail discount on the products, handles all the paperwork, and calls me when I need to pick them up; you can't get much better than that. And better yet, whenever I go into the store, they always remind me that I want to buy raisins for Chelsea and natural dog treats for Ubu.

—Judi

SHOPPING

We provide an extensive resource guide in the back of this book, which lists sources for essential oils and other aromatherapy products. Some of our friends, impressed with the results of the blends we created for them, ran to the nearest health-food store with their credit cards turbocharged. Several weeks later, they finally began to understand just how few drops and how few oils are needed for most recipes. Their bought-in-haste oils are now on display, gathering dust. Don't let this happen to you!

We recommend a starter kit of twelve oils that you can mix and match to create literally hundreds of blends. The starter kit includes at least one oil from each of the major oil groups (no, this is not like the four food groups, but you're close): wood/leaves/roots; flowers; herbs/spices; and citrus.

THE SEASONS STARTER KIT:	PRICE
Cedar	$4.80
Chamomile	$58.00
Clary Sage	$10.62
Eucalyptus	$3.48
Fennel	$5.86
Geranium	$9.42
Lavender	$7.26
Lemon	$4.80
Orange	$3.00
Peppermint	$5.74
Rosemary	$5.80
Tea Tree	$7.44
Total	$126.22

Note: *We include approximate wholesale prices in the list to give you an idea of your initial investment. Prices will vary depending on supplier. This list is based on prices for ½-oz. quantities.*

THE ESPECIALLY FOR YOU KIT	PRICE
Rose (Attar)	$8.95
Jasmine (Grandiflorum)	$9.74
Bergamot	$1.87
Patchouli	$1.99
Myrrh	$4.02
Sandalwood (Tamil Nadu)	$5.11
Neroli	$12.52
Ylang-Ylang	$2.56
Vanilla (Surfine Extra)	$7.28
Clove	$1.41
Frankincense	$3.98
Rosewood	$1.58
Total	$64.50

Note: These prices are based on quantities of .12 ounce.

In addition to buying the essential oils, you will want to purchase one or more vegetable or nut oils to use as a blending base. We think that:

- Olive oil is great for hair and body blends,

- Sweet almond oil works for face, sensitive skin areas, and blends for children, and

෴ Canola oil (which is absorbed into the skin most quickly of all base oils) can be used for all other blends that require a base oil.

So for less than $200, you can start your journey to a better way of healing and living.

THE OTHER BOOK
YOU SHOULD HAVE

We highly recommend Valerie Ann Worwood's *The Complete Book of Essential Oils and Aromatherapy* (New World Library, 1991). We refer to this book as our bible, and take it with us when we travel. It presents scientific facts along with charts of most essential oils and their uses, is written in a very easy-to-read manner, and answers just about every practical aromatherapy question we've had.

MAKING
YOUR BLENDS

As with any recipe, make sure you have all ingredients before you start. It also makes sense to have a nice work area.

෴ *At first, I made blends on an as-needed basis. Now, once a month, I dedicate one morning to creating my frequently used blends and experimenting with new ones.*

—Judi

❧ At first I took over the kitchen, stored my oils in a dry, dark cupboard, and probably spent a three- to four-hour session once a month to make the things I ran out of. Now, whenever I run out of a blend, I make more of the essential oil combination than I need at that time. I store the extra in a dark glass bottle. This gives me a head start next time I run out of something. Then I just add the oil, water, or other mixer.

—Paula

Once you have all the ingredients and a place to create your blends, acquiring containers to use for storing fresh blends can be quite challenging.

❧ I recruited new parents to bring me their baby food jars. Although the caps don't reseal tightly, I simply reinforced the tops with a piece of masking tape. I removed the labels, replacing them with a label on the jar (not the lid) as to the content and usage of the blend.

Now I have sturdy glass jars in which to make and store blends.

—Judi

Warning: Never put any essential oil in your eyes, and always wash your hands after working with oils so you don't accidentally rub some into your eyes.

STORAGE

Since most oils come in a dark glass bottle, be careful to keep your oils in a "non-breakable" area of your home.

❦ *For those of you with toddlers, like me, it's the top shelf of the linen closet behind a locked door.*

—Judi

❦ *I found this great old wooden cutlery tray that I keep my oils in. I store the attractive closed case in my kitchen. The case keeps out light and moisture, and keeps the oils convenient.*

—Paula

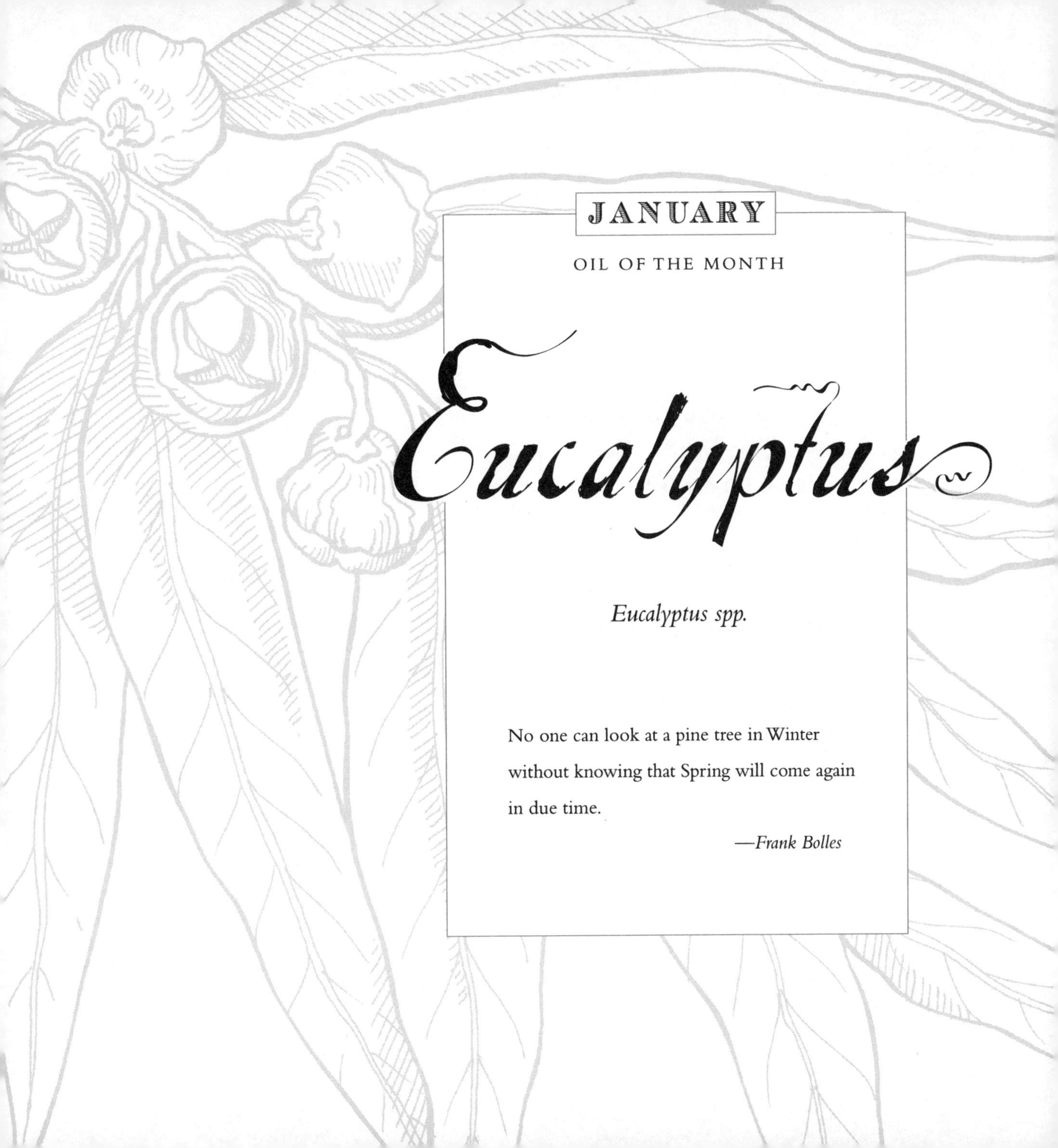

OIL OF THE MONTH

Eucalyptus

Eucalyptus spp.

No one can look at a pine tree in Winter
without knowing that Spring will come again
in due time.

—*Frank Bolles*

happy new year

freezing cold, frozen like ice

hot cocoa, warm fireplace

mittens, hats, and boots

slush, scrapers, Rudolph noses

after-holiday sales

new beginnings

Being First

There are many pressures associated with being first, as you firstborns know, as first-place winners know, and as January knows. There are expectations that *first* means best, that one must stay first, and that others are allowed to closely scrutinize your actions.

January does *first* in its own capricious way. Everyone has a great story about January—their blizzard-blessed ski trip, a classic Times Square New Year's Eve party, or the sizzling winter vacation they took to a warmer climate. This month is filled with possibility; however, with just about every great thing that happens in January, there is some little *worst* that can also happen. The worst cold, the worst sore throat, the worst muscle strains, the worst cough—all these can rear their ugly heads in January too.

Our job is to enjoy the very best of January and be armed and dangerous to fight off the worst. That is why Eucalyptus is such a terrific oil for January. When you think of Eucalyptus, you often think of a cool, cleansing smell. But the wonderful aroma of Eucalyptus is only the beginning. You can use Eucalyptus, with its many healing properties, to attack the worsts.

Eucalyptus

Crush a Eucalyptus leaf and take a deep, cleansing breath— you travel to a state of mind that is clear, crisp, alive. You are experiencing why eucalyptus is a top note in oil blending. Since the eighteenth century, Eucalyptus has been distilled for use in chest problems. Doctors John White and Dennis Cossiden identified this versatile plant in the Blue Mountains of New South Wales, Australia. These mountains got their name from the extraordinary blue haze that exudes from the resin of the eucalyptus trees.

Eucalyptus is a strong plant with a well-developed root system that grows quickly and has abundant vitality; it secretes oils into the soil to prevent other plants from growing in the immediate vicinity. The branches of the tree are shaped like a human lung, and this is the area of the body that Eucalyptus is most effective in treating. It's great for respiratory problems.

Eucalyptus oil, which is extracted from the leaves and twigs of Eucalyptus trees, has a strong, medicinal smell that is crisp and powerful. In addition to its outstanding fragrance, Eucalyptus' most dramatic characteristic is its versatility. It acts as an anti-inflammatory, antiseptic, antibiotic, antiviral, analgesic, and diuretic. Eucalyptus is so adaptable that it can be used to cool the body in the summer and warm it in winter.

Eucalyptus enjoys a successful reputation in the cold and flu world; it is an agreeable oil for all the ills of January. It also activates the red blood cells that increase oxygen to every cell in the body, and is used in the treatment of sprains and pains.

And finally, Eucalyptus is great for giving you a sense of balance, calming your nervous system, and increasing concentration, which helps you think clearly and logically. With Eucalyptus, you feel physically and mentally healthy and vital. So join us as we explore many terrific ways you can add Eucalyptus to your life.

Remedies

You might think that Eucalyptus is best used when inhaled, and that is certainly its most obvious use. However, it is also very effective in baths, diffusers, and room sprays as well as in a massage oil. We have included several methods of use in many of these recipes, so read carefully to find a treatment plan that makes the most sense for you.

You'll also be happy to hear that Eucalyptus is effective in treating stomachaches and diarrhea, is a terrific oil for children, and has a deodorizing and germ-killing place in housecleaning efforts.

One of the most interesting things you'll notice in these recipes is that you can use the same combination of oils to treat a variety of ailments. This is not a typographical error; it just goes to show how versatile these oils are in working with you for overall health and well-being.

LITTLE CHILDREN, BIG COLDS

From the middle of October until the end of March, the single most advertised medical condition on television is the common cold. Whether it is "my throat is on fire," "get twenty-four-hour relief," or "the so-you-can-rest medicine," millions of dollars are spent on describing one of the worst and most frequent ailments we all suffer from.

The following recipe has multiple uses, so read the instructions to find the method or methods that best meet your needs. Keep in mind that this kids' cold-combating recipe can be used on children as young as two years old.

We all know that when one person gets a cold, they are usually generous enough to share it with the entire family. So at the first sign of a sniffle, I run for the Eucalyptus.

—*Judi*

CHILDREN'S COLD CURE

10 **drops Eucalyptus**

10 **drops Lavender**

10 **drops Tea Tree**

Mix all oils together. Use in any or all of the following ways:

- ↝ Put 3 drops in a diffuser at bedtime. In the morning, if the cold still stifles your child's breathing, clean the diffuser and add 3 drops to clean water.

- ↝ For heavy congestion during the night, put 2 drops on a piece of cotton and tuck it inside your resting child's pillowcase.

- ↝ Put 2 drops in a bath. Not only will the steam help clear nasal passages, but the calming properties of this blend will help your child rest.

↬ Add 3 drops to 2 teaspoons of vegetable oil, and massage the child's lung area (chest and back).

FOR FEVERS

Add 2 drops of this blend to a quart of tepid water. Use it to give your child a sponge bath every couple of hours.

Note: As with all ailments, be sure to contact your physician.

BIG CHILDREN, BIG COLDS

When it comes to colds, we all want the constant loving attention that children receive when they are sick. We want the window closed—no, opened; we want a drink of water—no, tea; we want soft tissues, soothing words, and lots of TLC. In this next recipe, TLC could mean Total Loss of Colds. Again, the same powerful ingredients have multiple uses, so find the combination that works best for the bigger baby when he or she is sick.

Why is it that we don't seem to have the same patience with our big patients as we do with our children? Well, that's another mystery for us to ponder when we have a moment free from running to the sick ward.

—Judi

ADULT COLD CURE

2 drops Eucalyptus

5 drops Geranium

3 drops Peppermint

5 drops Rosemary

Mix all oils together. Use in any or all of the following ways:

- Put 3 drops in a diffuser at bedtime. Children are not the only people to benefit from steam inhalation.

- Put 2 drops on a tissue and carry with you for a brief blast of relief.

- Put 4 drops in a bath. Not only will the steam help clear nasal passages, but the calming properties of this blend will help you rest.

- Add 8 drops to 2 tablespoons of vegetable oil, and massage the lung area (chest and back), neck, around the ears, forehead, nose, and cheekbones.

FEVER-ADE

Add 5 drops of Lavender to the blend above, and put 4 drops of the blend into a nice, warm bath. What a soothing way to help with a fever.

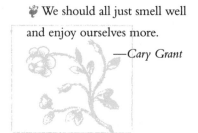

We should all just smell well and enjoy ourselves more.

—*Cary Grant*

THE CLEANSING SPRITZ OF HEALTH

If you have ever spent time investigating the common cold, you have heard the following: Wash hands after each sneeze, wash hands after contact with others, wash all items in the house that come into contact with germs. Well, there are only so many hours in a person's day—and the germs seem to work twenty-four-hour shifts.

We can't promise that Eucalyptus will make your home sterile, nor can we promise that you won't cringe every time someone sneezes in your child's face, but we can promise that the next recipe, which is like a spray of fresh air, will give you a fighting chance against germs that infiltrate your home.

Smells are surer than sounds and sights to make the heartstrings crack.

—*Rudyard Kipling*

COMMON COLD ANTISEPTIC SPRAY

3 drops Eucalyptus

4 drops Lavender

7 drops Lemon

2 drops Rosemary

2 drops Tea Tree

Mix all oils together. Add 8 drops of the blend to 1 quart of water.

Use this spray to clean floors and surfaces, disinfect germy areas, such as toys, and cleanse every nook and cranny, calming and cleaning as it goes.

This blend is great because you are cleaning your house and fighting colds in one spritz.

DID YOU KNOW?

Another benefit of Eucalyptus in a room spray is that it is great for reducing the desire to smoke, so take full advantage.

Especially for You

Battle the blues
Light, brisk scent for dark, cold days
Uplift and soothe

Post-holiday blues are as predictable as standing in the gift-return line at the department store. There is a wide variety of wonderful herbal, diet, and exercise strategies that work well to combat these feelings. You can also add a little rhythm to your blues with Bergamot. With its light, citrusy scent and mood-enhancing qualities, Bergamot is great for January.

The Bergamot tree, fragile cousin to orange and lemon trees, bears a fruit whose rinds are used for making Bergamot essential oil. This Italian tree provides an essential oil that is refreshing, gentle, and flowery. And as you would expect, Bergamot helps uplift and refresh your mind as well as your body.

SPRITZ YOUR SPIRITS

Make a body spray from a cup of water into which you add 2 drops of Bergamot and 2 drops of Lavender.

Use it any time you feel you're drooping.

ONE, TWO, I HAVE THE FLU

❦ *I get exhausted just remembering these moments. But as tired as I am dealing with colds, there is nothing like the fear of dealing with the flu. When that thermometer streaks up past the comfort level, our hearts go out to our patients and we are on alert.*

—*Judi*

Three, four, that's what Eucalyptus is for. Colds and coughs are tiring enough, but the flu can really grind a household to a halt. You sit in steamy bathrooms trying to get your exhausted child to drink more fluids, you run around the house with tea, soup, and tissues, you prop up innumerable pillows and put clean sheets on myriad sickbeds. At flu time all you want is one moment of that peace and quiet that comes when there is not a cough to be heard. So call on the arsenal of Eucalyptus, Lavender, Peppermint, and Rosemary to be your flu-fighters.

And if you thought you had some big babies when the bigger people in your house had a cold, you ain't seen nothing yet.

FLU-FIGHTERS

6 drops Eucalyptus

4 drops Lavender

2 drops Peppermint

2 drops Rosemary

❦ *Brian missed most of the Christmas festivities his first year in college because he had the flu—and was far from his mom's aromatherapy arsenal. According to him, he really had the Black Plague!*
—*Paula*

Mix all oils together. Use in any or all of the following ways:

- ↬ Put 3 drops in a diffuser.
- ↬ Put 2 drops in a bath.

◦ Add 3 drops to 2 teaspoons of vegetable oil, and
massage onto lung area (chest and back).

OH, MY ACHING BACK

Whether it was the strenuous exercise from running around
day and night caring for the infirm, or the aches and pains
you got from your overextended day on the slopes, muscle
aches are a year-round affliction. The next recipe is great for
taking the strain and pain away. You can really feel the blend
warm and relax those overworked, underused muscles.

❦ I love sledding, the cold air, the bright snow, the feeling of flying down the hill in anticipation of the tumble in the snowbank at the end. It's the long walk back up the hill, dragging the sled time and time again, that I could do without.

—Judi

———————— ❧ ❦ ————————

MUSCLE STRAIN REMEDY

10 drops **Eucalyptus**

10 drops **Peppermint**

10 drops **Rosemary**

Mix all oils together. Use in any of these ways:

◦ Put 10 drops into 2 tablespoons of vegetable oil and
massage the affected area. The ideal time to do this is
after a warm bath and before bedtime.

◦ Put 8 drops into a bath. Relax your cares away while
you deep soak the strain from your muscles.

Especially for You

Bergamot's uplifting scent is a great way to start your new year in the world of aromatherapy. When gift-exchange gets you frazzled, use the following blend.

RETURN AND RELAX

Put 4 drops of Bergamot, 4 drops of Lavender, and 2 drops of Clary Sage into a warm bath. Close the door, slide in, and relax for ten to fifteen minutes. Notice how calm and centered you feel afterwards.

a Yew Tree

More Sources of Eucalyptus

Eucalyptus is most frequently used to treat colds and their accompanying symptoms: hacking coughs, runny noses, and sore throats.

You can enjoy the benefits of Eucalyptus in other ways as well. Eucalyptus cough drops can be found in most grocery and drug stores; you can find dried boughs of Eucalyptus leaves at craft stores; or you can take a craft class and make your own Eucalyptus wreath.

Fill a basket with pine cones sprayed with Eucalyptus and you have a festive basket that helps keep you well all winter long.

The people who first developed Vicks VapoRub™ and liniment already knew a lot about Eucalyptus' good work for breathing and muscle relaxing.

If you like Eucalyptus, you might also like Naiouli or Camphor essential oils. Naiouli is from the leaves and twigs of another Australian plant, this one a shrub. It smells similar to Eucalyptus, and works well for bacterial infections, sore throats, and respiratory problems. Camphor, which is from the wood of an Asian tree, was used in old-time preparations for coughs and colds.

🌿 The ordinary arts we practice every day at home are of more importance to the soul than their simplicity might suggest.

—*Thomas Moore*

OIL OF THE MONTH

Lemon

Citrus limon

If we did not know the [lemon]—if someone
were suddenly to spring upon us a blossom of
exquisite ivory color and wonderful perfume,
which presently developed into a golden globe,
whose very rind was odorous, whose hue was a
glory—with what rapture we should receive it.

—*May Byron*

midwinter blues

cozy, warm kitchens looking out over dark, icy fields

thermal underwear, socks, and more socks

hearts and lace

sledding

shortest month, darkest month, lovers' month

new romance to warm the heart

The Short and Sweet Month

February, the shortest month of the year, has a dual personality. It's filled with holidays and a school vacation, great times to celebrate and share with those you love. It's also the month in the very deepest of winter, and can feel so cold and dark.

With Valentine's Day, Presidents' Day, and school vacation, there's plenty of time for winter sports and their accompanying aches and pains. After all, whose muscles are really ready for pulling those three kids up the hill on the toboggan or falling off it one more time? You'll need more energy now, and possibly a long aromatic soak in the tub later.

Valentine's Day is always a favorite holiday, with its beautiful colors, ruby red and snow white; its delicious flavors, chocolate and cherries; and its luxurious aromas, roses and fireplaces.

But the rest of life continues: work or school, errands, your cooped-up house that hasn't had an open window in way too long. That air is apt to be a little stale by now—not a welcome thought. So you will welcome Lemon, the oil for February, with its uplifting, cleansing, and energizing qualities.

The scent of Lemon is found to be joyful, light, and purifying. Think of it as the golden gift from the sun, which can be especially helpful during this month. Could anything counteract more completely the very depth of winter than Lemon? It is thought to bring brightness, optimism, and vitality into your life.

Lemon will help you bring a great mental feeling of warmth and rejuvenation to your home and family. So make February a sunshiny, lemony month to warm and up-lift you and your family.

Lemon

Lemon oil comes from the rind of the lemon. Its scent is much like that of the fruit: intense, sharp, clean, and citrusy. Lemon oil is often an additive in laundry and household cleaning supplies because of its clean and healthy smell.

Lemon seems to bring with it the very character of the places where it grows. Lemon trees were said to be first discovered in India. Over the centuries, they were intro-duced to other warm countries, such as Italy and Spain, and later to California and Florida.

Early sea travelers stocked up on fresh lemons and limes before a long voyage to prevent scurvy and to purify the ship's drinking water.

Both the smell and appearance of Lemon point to its strengths: concentration, cleansing, and mental warming. Lemon oil is an excellent aid to concentration, helping you to focus your thoughts. It is antibacterial, antiseptic, and antifungal, making it an excellent treatment for colds, sore throats, and flu-like conditions. It helps stimulate your immune system, and is also helpful in treating fevers—either suck a lemon (think of that without your eyes watering) or make a spray of the essential oil in water and spray the sickroom. This oil is a must-have for the cold and flu season.

Some of its beauty applications were rediscovered in California in the 1960s. Its ability to clean and lighten hair, especially for blondes, makes it useful in shampoos and hair rinses. Lemon is also helpful for dealing with dandruff.

Lemon is one of the adaptogens, a group of essential oils which can adapt their properties to suit your needs. For instance, lemon can relax you when you are stressed, yet energize you when you are tired.

Remedies

One of the easiest and least intrusive methods of using essential oils is in an air spray. This makes a lot of sense when using Lemon. We offer several air sprays in this chapter.

Baths are also a most effective and comfort-inducing way to use oils, especially for muscular aches and pains.

And then there is topical application, usually in a base oil. For Spot Mix, apply the oils straight, but very carefully and sparingly.

🌿 Smell is a potent wizard that transports us across thousands of miles and all the years we have lived.

—*Helen Keller*

Warning: Lemon increases photosensitivity of the skin, so do not apply before exposure to direct sunlight—probably not a problem this month, unless you live in the southern hemisphere.

Warning: *Lemon oil can cause skin irritation, so do not exceed 1 percent in any recipe. Always dilute Lemon oil.*

NATURE'S BEST BREAKFAST

The causes of "irregularity" are many: stress, virus, reaction to a particular food, or perhaps even a change in your mood or the season. Whatever the cause, the symptoms are the same and you are left feeling downright uncomfortable.

————————   ————————

BIRCHER MUESLI

1 tablespoon oats

3 tablespoons water or apple juice

1 tablespoon evaporated milk or soya milk

1 tablespoon grated or whole nuts

1 large grated apple with the peel

1 drop Lemon

Soak the oats overnight in the apple juice or water, in the refrigerator. Before breakfast, grate the apple and add with the rest of the ingredients.

You can also try a tablespoon of lemon juice in a glass of hot water to start your day off with renewed energy while dealing with that condition we don't like to talk about—irregularity!

Don't even mention the word constipation to me. When I was pregnant I tried everything from prunes to powders, and it was a muesli created by the Bircher Benner clinic in Zurich which includes Lemon that saved me.

—Judi

I think the lemon juice drink makes my teeth feel funny, so I always brush right after.

—Paula

Especially for You

Petals cover you
Warm blends for cold evenings
Soft and silky scent

Rose, of course, that most romantic of scents, is the special oil for February. Originally from Persia and India, rose is symbolic of love, peace, sex, and beauty. The builder of the Taj Mahal knew the value of Rose and filled his moats with rose petals on the day of his marriage to show his love for his new bride. Extracted from the very petals of the flowers given by the dozens this month, essential Rose oil is even better than the flower. It doesn't wilt and die at the end of the month, but can live through all the seasons of your love.

ROSES FOR ROMANCE

Buy as many unscented candles as you want to place on the dining room table or on your bed's headboard. Put a drop of Rose directly on the top of each candle, light, and enjoy!

COLD AND FLU SEASON–STILL

As you know, merely making it through January with a flu-free household doesn't mean flu season is over. Lemon, the oil of the month for February, is also effective in dealing with symptoms of the flu.

You can use lemon juice to make a pleasant, though tart, mouthwash and gargle. Often a sore throat is the first sign of worse symptoms to come. The following gargle can be very effective in both alleviating pain and fighting those nasty germs that have already invaded your throat. It also helps against that nasty breath that sick people often get.

Trying to teach a child how to spit the gargle out without swallowing it was so much fun that my daughter almost forgot she was sick. However, we had to discuss rules on spitting before it got out of hand.

—Judi

RECIPE FOR LEMON GARGLE

2 drops Lavender

2 drops Lemon

1 teaspoon salt

1 teaspoon baking soda

Mix all ingredients into glass of warm water. Gargle until it is all gone.

For a nice, hot drink that is very soothing to a sore throat, try Lemon-Lavender Toddy: Add one tablespoon honey and one tablespoon lemon juice to a mug of hot water. Add a drop of Lavender for a comforting tea.

OUT, DAMNED SPOT!

Even when you take great care of your skin, you still get the occasional blemish.

Dealt with improperly, a little inflammation can preface something more serious. And we all know you don't break out when it doesn't matter, it happens right before an important social event or a major presentation.

Try a little dab of this Blemish Blocker on your next pimple. You can feel it go right to work. This works especially well on teenaged skin.

Funny, Judi, with her great-looking skin, didn't know what a "spot" was. My teenaged son knew right away!

—*Paula*

Wouldn't you know, as soon as I learned about this blend, I needed it!

—*Judi*

BLEMISH BLOCKER

10 drops Lavender

10 drops Lemon

10 drops Tea Tree

Mix all the oils together and store in a dark glass container. Use the end of cotton swab to apply tiny amounts to blemishes on your skin.

This may sting when you apply it. Don't use it too often, because it is also very drying. But say good-bye to those spots!

Last week, I had a facial and mentioned facial spots to the aesthetician. I said it always seems like everybody is looking at only the spot when they talk to me. She didn't help alleviate that fear; she said, "They probably are!"

—*Paula*

JUST A DROP

You might also try a drop of Lemon essential oil on an insect bite or a cat scratch. It helps keep down swelling and takes away the itch while disinfecting the skin.

BRIGHT OR EARLY

This is the time of year when you would rather unplug that alarm and roll over to sleep until spring than get out of bed in the morning. You can be up bright or early, but not both.

To make it a bit easier to rise, try this energizing air spray wherever you spend the first minutes of your morning.

ENERGY SPRAY

1 drop Lavender

4 drops Lemon

3 drops Orange

2 drops Rosemary

Mix the oils into 3 cups of water. Spray around your home and work area for an energy lift.

If you're like me, the first few minutes in the morning are spent begging the coffee maker to hurry up.
—Judi

If you liked the recipe for Energy Spray (and why wouldn't you?), mix up several batches of the essential oils and store in a dark glass bottle. Then you have most of the work done whenever you need more spray.

CLEARING THE AIR

Germs are probably at their worst in February, and inside air is at its stuffiest. In trying to keep your surroundings warm, you have probably turned your back on fresh air (at least in the house).

Try the sprays in this section to take advantage of Lemon's disinfecting action. It's particularly good at the office. A problem of the workplace in today's tight office buildings is the ease with which we share germs. All it takes is one sick person in a six-person office, and you often have five coughing, hacking families. Use this spray to cut down on those statistics:

ANTISEPTIC AIR SPRAY

1 drop Eucalyptus

2 drops Lavender

3 drops Lemon

2 drops Tea Tree

This spray is great for household use as well, to clean and disinfect at the same time.

—*Judi*

Add to 3 cups water. Use as an air spray or as a surface disinfectant. Don't forget to spray telephones, which look so innocent but can harbor germs.

Lemon oil also is said to offset confusion and distraction. Sound anything like you during those low-energy points of the day? Like after that post-lunch planning meeting in the middle of the afternoon?

Lemon, which is considered a rational oil, has been used to increase worker productivity. Try this air spray to become an efficiency expert with more mental clarity and decisiveness:

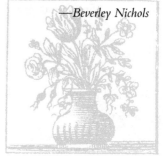

CONCENTRATION SPRAY

3 drops Lemon

2 drops Peppermint

3 drops Rosemary

Add oils to 2 cups water. Spray around your work area when you find your mental energy flagging, or for that after-lunch sleepiness.

LEMONIZE YOUR HOUSE

There's another way to fill your home with the scent of lemons: Make your own furniture polish. Now, we realize your time for housework is at a premium, but you want your home to be as welcoming as possible. Just try the recipe for homemade furniture polish and see if you don't love the difference. You'll notice a clean and fresh smell to the whole room that is somehow old-fashioned and may evoke some childhood memory.

———————————— ℰ ℱ ————————————

NOSTALGIC FURNITURE POLISH

4 ounces linseed oil

4 ounces white vinegar

24 drops Lemon

12 drops Lavender

Mix this up just like salad dressing, shaking before each application. Spray onto furniture or apply with a soft cloth. Rub into your wood furniture, polishing it to a nice shine.

LEISURE TIME

Just because it's wintertime doesn't mean people stop playing sports. And it also doesn't mean that you won't get hurt by pushing muscles beyond their present ability.

Muscles pushed to do things they haven't done in awhile deserve the following relaxing sports massage after a warm bath. You might prefer to have someone else rub the Muscle-Relaxing Massage into your tired, aching muscles—preferably someone with warm hands.

Skiing does it to me. I always think I'm in good enough shape and don't need to stretch out before my first run of the day, or I go for one more run than I really should.

—Paula

RECIPE FOR A MUSCLE-RELAXING MASSAGE

12 drops Lavender

12 drops Lemon

9 drops Peppermint

9 drops Rosemary

Mix all essential oils into 2 tablespoons olive oil. Keep at room temperature, or slightly warmer.

For those who don't have the time or inclination after their winter sports for a muscle-soothing bath (the campfire and hot chocolate beckon, no doubt), try something quicker just before a shower:

PRE-SHOWER MUSCLE RUB

Use any three of the following essential oils: Cedar, Clary Sage, Eucalyptus, Lemon, Orange, or Rosemary. Add one drop of each selected oil to a warm, wet washcloth. Rub large-muscle areas—arms, shoulders, legs, and buttocks—with the cloth. Shower as usual. Avoid rubbing the oils into or onto your eyes, genitals, or mucous membranes.

Brave your storm with firm endeavor, let your vain repinings go! Hopeful hearts will find forever Roses underneath the snow!

—*Cooper*

Or if you have the time before you start your athletics, try a pre-sport aromatic bath.

RECIPE FOR PRE-SPORT BATH

2 drops Chamomile

3 drops Lavender

4 drops Lemon

3 drops Rosemary

Add these essential oils to a warm bath. Soak in the tub as a prelude to stretching.

And while you are in the shower, try this rinse, which is especially effective for our light-haired friends:

RINSE FOR LIGHT HAIR

15 drops Cedar

10 drops Lemon

Mix oils together and add to 8 ounces of liquid hair conditioner.

Apply as you would any conditioner after you have rinsed out the shampoo from your hair.

❦ If I give you a rose, you will not doubt of God.
—*Clement of Alexander*

If You Like Lemons, Make Lemonade

Your mouth starts watering at the mere thought of sinking your teeth into the rind of a lemon, and you probably pucker up, too. This oil's light citrus scent makes you think of clean air and warm sunshine, and Lemon is excellent in helping you concentrate and focus.

One of the simplest arrangements for your table is a bowl of lemons. A white or blue bowl filled with lemons goes just as far as flowers in cheering a room. You can add any bits of greenery you may have around, or other colors with fruit (beautiful red apples) or candles (forest green candle with a white ribbon).

And even after the lemons look less inviting, you can still make use of their oil and juice. Quarter a lemon and grind it up in your garbage disposal. Chase it with hot water. This cleans and disinfects the garbage disposal as well as scenting the kitchen.

If your little Mother's helpers want to help with dusting, Lemon oil in water is a safe and effective way to clean countertops, windows, and bathroom fixtures.

Don't Forget Cupid

Use essential oils to make special gifts for Valentine's Day. My daughter's daycare provider loved the little heart-shaped sachet we made. Chelsea cut out a heart-shaped piece of felt

Especially for You

Give yourself and those close to you the gift of Rose! Valentine's Day can be painful for those who have no partners. Rose oil is antidepressant and calming, gentle enough for a baby. Make your single friends or yourself feel special with this next blend.

FEELING GOOD ABOUT YOU

Make a room spray of 4 drops of Rose, 2 drops of Bergamot, and 2 drops of Lavender in a cup of water. Spray away the loneliness and experience the love that surrounds you.

A rose is a rose is a rose.

—*Gertrude Stein*

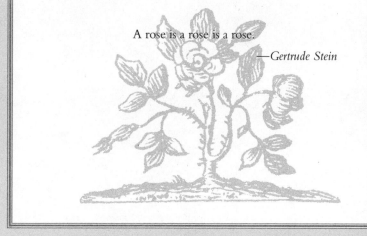

(okay, it didn't really look like a heart) and I put a few drops of Lemon oil on it. The teacher kept it in her desk, and whenever she needed a boost of energy, she would take it out and smell it.

If you like Lemon essential oil, you might also like Grapefruit, Lime, Citronella, or Lemongrass essential oils. Grapefruit and Lime are made just like Lemon essential oil: they are expressed from the peels and will smell just as you expect. Citronella is made from a grass grown in Madagascar and South America. You may remember the scent of Citronella from sitting outside on early summer evenings. It's quite effective in warding off mosquitoes. Lemongrass essential oil is made from the leaves of Lemongrass, a grass-type plant used in Asian cooking. It has a rich, lemony-ginger scent.

🌿 Luxury need not have a price—comfort itself is a luxury.
—*Geoffrey Beene*

OIL OF THE MONTH

Cedrus atlantica

No matter what changes take place in the
world, or in me, nothing ever seems to disturb
the face of spring.

—*E. B. White*

no more snow—please

temperatures sneak above 40°

strong wind makes me feel like I can fly

melting ice drips crystals in the March sun

I really have to get my tax material together

anticipating the birth of a new season

skiing is at its best in March

A Time of Transition

Transitions are a wonderful experience in which we pass from one phase into another. We all remember, sometimes with much embarrassment, our transition through puberty — our lives were never the same. We also remember the excitement of getting our license, thus making the transition into yet another phase of our life—independence! Take a moment and think about the significant transitions in your life, some great memories, some painful events, yet you moved forward and grew.

That's how it is with the month of March, one of the more outstanding transition months. We have been hibernating for the past several months, looking out icy windows and sitting in front of warm fires. We have been praying that our car batteries didn't freeze overnight, and our children are praying for a snow day off from school.

March makes a blustery introduction, with its strong, chilly winds and sun glare reflected off snow-covered patches of ground. Like an actor in a Shakespearean play, it bounds out onto stage and dramatically draws you into his or her feelings. As the actor comes to the heartbreaking close of his soliloquy, we pause to take a deep breath and look ahead. March does the same thing by wrapping its windy arms around us and carrying us into its drama, only to be placed gracefully back on the ground with the birth of April right around the corner.

🕊 Begin now doing what you want to do now. We are not living in eternity. We have only this moment, sparkling like a star in our hand—and melting like a snowflake.

—*Marie Beynon Ray*

Cedar is a great oil for this month because it helps to heal skin and hair that have been hibernating and because it has an emotional effect that leaves you feeling grounded, supported, and prepared.

Warning: Some of the properties of some Cedar (not the one recommended in this book) may have abortive effects, and thus no Cedar should be used in any form during pregnancy. Because Cedar contains thuyon, it should never be taken orally.

Cedar

Like most essential oils that are extracted from wood, wood chips, or the sawdust of trees, Cedar is a majestic oil. It acts as a symbol of strength, dignity, and nobility. Just stand beneath a Cedar tree and you are awed by its impressive height and strength. These trees are abundant in North America and North Africa.

Cedar has a warm, musky, balsamic fragrance that is long-lasting and quite effective in holding blends together. This earthy scent makes you feel solidly grounded and supported.

Cedar's reputation as an essential oil is built upon two major attributes. First, it does wonderful things for hair and skin; second, it has a calming, balancing effect on your mental and emotional state.

Because of this calming characteristic, Cedar is excellent as an antidote for environmental stress caused by excessive lighting, noise, and cramped working conditions. A drop of

Cedar on the bulb of your desk lamp, for example, will create a little protective barrier between you and work-related stress.

Cedar also acts very well as an insect repellent and in treating bronchial problems, although Eucalyptus and Peppermint are so strong in those two areas that Cedar is often overlooked.

So think of this month as a time of regrouping, moving from winter to spring, and establishing a mental state that helps calm during times of fear and nervous tension. Focus on stabilizing your energies and giving your heart courage. Bravely meet the new season.

Remedies

Cedar is most often used in massage blends. Whether you are massaging your scalp, your skin, your hair, or your upset stomach, Cedar blends work well.

Another enjoyable way to use Cedar is in a diffuser or room spray to help you gain a sense of balance and wholeness. Its fragrance is often associated with the autumn and winter holidays of Halloween, Thanksgiving, and Christmas; a few squirts from a Cedar spray can bring back fond recollections of those holidays.

❧ People from a planet without flowers would think we must be mad with joy the whole time to have such things about us.

—*Iris Murdoch*

HAIR TODAY, GONE TOMORROW

Hair loss is one of those transitions that most of us face with a grimace, and a vengeance to combat the passing of our golden locks. Who wants to grow old gracefully?

So let's see how Cedar can help with this transition. We have one recipe designed to give the scalp an uplifting and strengthening boost, and a second recipe that deals with the specific issue of hair loss.

USE THE BEST

When you blend a new hair treatment, olive oil is the best base oil to use.

———————————— ❧ ❧ ————————————

RECIPE FOR SCALP TREATMENT

2 drops Cedar

4 drops Lavender

1 drop Lemon

2 drops Rosemary

2 drops Tea Tree

Mix all oils together in 2 tablespoons of olive oil. Use the entire blend to massage into scalp thoroughly. Wrap your head with a towel and relax for one hour. Shampoo and rinse—you may have to do this twice to remove all the olive oil.

Another benefit of the above recipe is that the essential oils are wonderful for stabilizing your emotions and letting you escape from anger, fear, and aggression. So even if you already have a healthy scalp and hair, treat your emotions to the blend.

Paula turned me on to this first recipe. I use it at least once a month to give my scalp some special attention. Her recipe called for some oils that we do not feature in this book, so I modified it a bit and tried it for three months, and feel that we still have a winning blend here because my hair has a glossy shine.

—Judi

Especially for You

Seeking earth's embrace
Rainy forest primeval
Soft, soft rain cries down

Myrrh is one of the most ancient aromatic substances known. The Egyptians imported it to use as offerings to honor their deities. Myrrh essential oil is made from the gum resin of the Commiphora myrrha tree, grown in Africa and Arabia. Myrrh's pleasant balsamic smell enhances spiritual meditations, helping you ground yourself and allowing you to focus in a relaxed way. It is also useful for healing "wounds of the heart."

Take advantage of the warmth and groundedness of Myrrh after a hectic day. Use the scent of Myrrh to brighten and warm yourself. Heat the essential oil alone in a lamp ring for a rich scent while you sit and relax. Take a few minutes with your eyes closed to still your thoughts. Use the following massage oil prior to yoga or slow stretching exercises.

STRETCH LIKE A CAT

Mix 4 drops Cedar, 1 drop Myrrh, 3 drops Sandalwood into one ounce canola oil. Rub this all over your skin before you start your slow exercises. The scent will slowly move around you as your skin heats up.

While men seem to be the most obvious group affected by hair loss, this is also a problem faced by females. Women who have over-processed their hair with perms, colors, and styling aids find that after a while their hair is brittle and subject to falling out after shampoos or brushing.

RECIPE FOR HAIR LOSS TREATMENT

3 drops Cedar

2 drops Clary Sage

2 drops Lemon

3 drops Rosemary

Mix all oils together in 2 tablespoons of olive oil. You can use this blend in two ways:

- Massage blend onto hair and scalp; make sure you reach those split ends. Wrap your head with a towel and relax for one hour. Shampoo and rinse. Be sure to rinse well to remove the olive oil.

- Add a few drops of this blend to a mild shampoo and use on a regular basis when you wash your hair.

DYNAMIC SPRAY

If you are feeling physically, emotionally, or mentally drained, don't let things drag you down. Make some

🍀 When I did some computer training in a hair salon, I learned as much about hair as the salon staff did about computers. The hair care specialists I spoke to helped me understand that there are many factors that effect the state of our hair, including hormonal changes, stress, dietary changes, and even seasonal changes.

They further explained that each person may face dandruff, oily, or dry hair at different times in their lives. So I said to Paula, "We'll have to include blends to address each hair care concern." And here they are!

—Judi

Dynamic Spray. Add 2 drops Orange, 2 drops Cedar, 2 drops Rosemary, and 2 drops Peppermint to a cup of water. Spritz your house and start feeling re-energized.

IT'S TOO DRY, TOO OILY, OR TOO FLAKY

There are so many shampoo and conditioning products on the market today that it can be overwhelming and confusing. And the number of commercials or advertisements that focus on hair care only make it more difficult to answer the question, "Which hair care product is best for me?" Hair care experts recommend that you change your shampoo on a regular basis, suggesting that your hair receives the greatest benefit by this variation.

RECIPE FOR DAMAGED HAIR TREATMENT

1 drop Cedar

3 drops Clary Sage

1 drop Geranium

1 drop Lavender

3 drops Rosemary

Mix all oils together in 2 tablespoons of olive oil. You can use this blend in one of two ways:

- Massage blend on hair and scalp; make sure you reach those split ends. Wrap your head with a towel and relax for one hour. Shampoo and rinse. Be sure to rinse well to remove the olive oil.

- Add a few drops of this blend to a mild shampoo and use on a regular basis when you wash your hair.

Warning: *Some of the properties of some Cedar (not the one recommended in this book) may have abortive effects, and thus no Cedar should be used in any form during pregnancy. Because Cedar contains thuyon, it should never be taken orally.*

DON'T BE SAD

Cedar, Clary Sage, and Lavender, used in the blend above, are also effective when you are grieving, feeling scattered, or can't sleep. Instead of massaging your scalp, you may want to use these oils in a room spray or diffuser.

Beauty more than bitterness makes the heart break.

—*Sara Teasdale*

Oily hair seems to be a condition of being a teenager, whether caused by hormonal changes or the extra sweat and energy used on sports. Seasonal changes can also cause hair to become oily, so here's a recipe to help.

RECIPE FOR OILY HAIR TREATMENT

3 drops Cedar

3 drops Lemon

3 drops Rosemary

Mix all oils together in 2 tablespoons of olive oil. You can use this blend in one of two ways:

- Massage blend into hair and scalp; make sure you reach those split ends. Wrap your head with a towel and relax for one hour. Shampoo and rinse. Be sure to rinse well to remove the olive oil.

- Add a few drops of this blend to a mild shampoo and use on a regular basis when you wash your hair.

QUIET-TIME SPRAY

One drop each of Cedar, Lemon, Lavender, and Orange makes a great room spray, especially for children's rooms. The calming and balancing effect of these oils helps slow down the overactive child.

When my daughter chose not to nurse any longer, I was free to experiment with these blends and found that they helped considerably until my hair returned to its healthy, shiny, natural wavy state.

—Judi

As unpredictable as oily hair can be, dandruff can also pop up when you least expect it. As hundreds of television commercials tell you, "You only have one chance to make a good first impression." So use the following blend if you find those undesirable flakes appearing on your shoulders.

RECIPE FOR DANDRUFF TREATMENT

3 drops Cedar

3 drops Rosemary

3 drops Tea Tree

Mix all oils together in 2 tablespoons of olive oil. You can use this blend in two ways:

- Massage blend into hair and scalp; make sure you reach those split ends. Wrap your head with a towel, and relax for one hour. Shampoo and rinse.
- Add a few drops of this blend to a mild shampoo and use on a regular basis when you wash your hair.

The place you are in needs you today.

—*Katherine Logan*

FROM HEAD TO TOE

Cedar is a terrific oil that treats your hair and skin to some tender loving care. The next recipe might surprise you because you have already seen it in this chapter for treating damaged hair.

I am one of those people who is affected by the change in seasons. My skin reacts to the change and I have to alter my skin moisturizer for each season. The same is true for my hair, my health, and my attitude. This recipe is my winter-to-spring blend.

—Judi

RECIPE FOR WINTER SKIN CARE

1 drop Cedar

3 drops Clary Sage

1 drop Geranium

1 drop Lavender

3 drops Rosemary

Mix all oils together in 2 tablespoons of olive oil. Massage your entire body with this relaxing blend. Don't forget those extra-dry areas, such as elbows, knees, and ankles.

For those of you whose skin reacts more dramatically, causing a form of dermatitis, we have a wonderful solution.

RECIPE FOR DERMATITIS DEMOLISHER

2 drops Cedar

3 drops Chamomile

3 drops Lavender

2 drops Tea Tree

Mix oils together. You can use this blend in two ways:

↬ Pour the blend into a bowl of steaming water, over which you put your face. For the greatest benefit, drape a towel over your head to contain the healing moisture.

↬ Mix blend into 2 tablespoons of a light oil, such as almond oil, and massage the affected skin areas.

Now let's turn our attention to a more sensual use of aromatherapy. Because Cedar provides calming, comforting, warming, and harmonious benefits, it is a must in a sensual massage blend. Give the following a try sometime, and enjoy! If you are by yourself, simply pour the blend into a nice warm bath, put on soothing music, and let your imagination float you away.

❧ I don't care how rotten my day was—as soon as I slip into a bath with the following blend, I am transported to a more relaxed, and even sexy, state of mind.

—Judi

—— ⅋ ——

RECIPE FOR SENSUAL AND RELAXING BATH

2 drops Cedar

2 drops Clary Sage

2 drops Lavender

2 drops Orange

Mix oils in 2 tablespoons of vegetable oil, and . . . (need we say more?)

Especially for You

March can be a weary month, with its leftover winter cold and darkness. Use the strengths of Myrrh, its warmth and comfort, to ease your mind and body. The Myrrh plant uses its oil as a protection against the sun in its natural desert habitat. And you can follow its lead in this skin rejuvenation blend. The gods would be jealous.

YOUTH AMULET FOR SKIN

2 drops Chamomile, 2 drops Clary Sage, 2 drops Myrrh, 8 drops Rosemary, and 8 drops Geranium. Blend the essential oils into 2 ounces of sweet almond oil or olive oil. Use this on your skin at night after you cleanse.

STARTS LIKE A LION, ENDS LIKE A LAMB

March has that reputation and we find that sometimes our "lion's" indulgences require some "lamb" care. Again, Cedar can help. Constipation—now there's a beast that requires gentle and immediate handling so you feel better sooner.

Too much food, too much alcohol, too much stress. Whenever I have the "too much" syndrome, the following blend is great!

—Judi

———————— ☙ ❧ ————————

OVERINDULGENCE REMEDY

5 drops Cedar

10 drops Lavender

5 drops Lemon

5 drops Peppermint

15 drops Rosemary

Mix oils in 2 tablespoons of vegetable oil and massage lower abdomen in a clockwise direction three times a day.

This blend can be used for several days until you're back to normal.

Warning: Because Cedar contains *thuyon, it should never be taken orally.*

Surround Yourself with Scent of Cedar

Cedar is a very calming oil, so don't forget to include it in baths.

Wouldn't we all like to have a cedar closet or chest for our clothes? Well, if you don't have a carpenter's touch, you can buy cedar chips to put into closets to keep your clothes free from moths and smelling fresh.

A wonderful table arrangement includes pine cones sprayed with Cedar, evergreens, and bright bows.

If you like Cedar, you might also like Sandalwood, Rosewood, or other woody essential oils. Sandalwood, often used in Asian perfumes, has a warm, spicy aroma. Rosewood, which has a sweeter scent than Cedar or Sandalwood, is relaxing but at the same time uplifting.

APRIL

OIL OF THE MONTH

Clary Sage

Salvia sclarea

April prepares her green traffic light and the
world thinks Go.

—*Christopher Morley*

a robin, perhaps

tiny little buds

teasingly warm days

finally opening windows

anticipation

what can we plant this year?

rain, rain, and more rain

exploring new running routes

spring cleaning

dear sun, warming my soul

I feel fresh, alive, new

At Last—Spring!

Who thought April would ever get here? Buds that struggled to stick their heads above the snow are now almost in full bloom. Newer, less hardy plants are now gathering the strength and courage to make their own journey toward the sun. And the sight of a robin fills you with delight and hope.

Although spring officially begins in March, you could never tell it from that cold, blustery, changeable month. We don't really feel spring-like until April arrives with her warm rains and breezes. Finally it seems a good idea to open the windows and air out the house. (Another good idea: take the percale sheets out of the linen closet and put the flannel sheets away until next winter.)

The excitement of newness and growth permeates us. We want to rejuvenate ourselves, shed the winter enclosures, and start on that list of things we waited for warm weather to do. With this energy can come overexertion and maybe a bit too much anticipation.

Clary Sage, the oil for April, is good to have as your companion for meeting the beginning of spring. It's relaxing and uplifting, good for new times and newly found energy, great for giving you an alive, vibrant feeling after the long dreary months of winter.

❧ No winter lasts forever, no spring skips its turn. April is a promise that May is bound to keep.

—*Hal Borland*

Clary Sage

Clary Sage essential oil is derived from the pink, blue, or purple blossoms of the clary (Salvia sclarea) plant. It is grown in Spain, Italy, and France. We think it smells like newly mown hay—not your typical floral scent. Others describe it as earthy, primitive, or musky.

Clary Sage's signature is the flower, which is very sensual and feminine-appearing, much like a Georgia O'Keefe painting. And the oil from the flower, not surprisingly, is excellent in dealing with women's ailments such as PMS and cramps, as well as working on the emotions.

Clary Sage is useful in dealing with strong emotions, such as fear, stress, and anxiety. It also has very relaxing properties; we like to think that the Wizard of Oz characters were running through a field of Clary Sage when they fell asleep. The relaxing qualities of Clary Sage also make it a very sensual oil.

On a physical level, it is great for mature or inflamed skin. It is also helpful in dealing with menstrual cramps and deep muscle tension. It is antiseptic, deodorizing, and anti-inflammatory.

That's why, in the remedies for this month, you will find ways to use Clary Sage for body rubs, as a way to relax, to ease menstrual cramps, alleviate a headache, fight off a bad mood, care for your skin and nails, and as a spray that lifts your mood.

🌺 *Once upon a time, I was crabby for no understandable reason (probably PMS) and had to drive two teenagers an hour and a half up to Massachusetts. Two drops of Clary Sage on a cotton ball near my side of the car calmed my bad mood and allowed me to enjoy their company.*

—Paula

Waring: Clary Sage should never be used by pregnant women or people with epilepsy. Use of it should not be combined with iron supplements or alcoholic beverages. Clary Sage is not made from the Sage plant (Salvia officinalis); however, the essential oil Sage is. The two are not interchangeable.

Remedies

Clary Sage works well in an oil base (such as sweet almond, canola, or olive oil) for a skin rub or massage. Diluted in milk or bath oil, it makes a relaxing bath. You can also combine Clary Sage with other essential oils, such as Geranium, Orange, or Lavender, for a relaxing soak in the tub.

Clary Sage is kind to skin, which is why we present it here for facial use. The more you work with this oil, the more you appreciate its decidedly feminine leaning.

🌺 *Not that I'd know anything about forty-something women, but I read that somewhere in a book.*
—*Paula*

🌺 *I must have read the same book—either that or my birth certificate.*
—*Judi*

BEST FACE FORWARD

The following recipe uses the anti-inflammatory tendencies of Clary Sage as well as its anti-wrinkle properties. Use this blend for a before-bed regimen that is good for your skin during this changeable month of April. The following recipe is especially good for women in their thirties and forties.

———————— ⚘ ⚘ ————————

RECIPE FOR ANTI-WRINKLE MOISTURIZER

6 drops Clary Sage

6 drops Fennel

4 drops Geranium

4 drops Lavender

Mix the essential oils together. Use in one or both of the
following ways:

- Add the blend to 2 tablespoons sweet almond oil or
  apricot kernel oil. Massage this mixture into a clean
  face before bedtime.

- Add the blend to 4 ounces distilled water or spring
  water and 1 ounce witch hazel and use it as a toner, in
  the morning and at night.

———————————————————

To keep skin clear through sweaty spring days when your
skin is trying to adjust to the change in seasons and
temperature, try the skin toner below.

———————— ⚘ ⚘ ————————

RECIPE FOR SPRING TONER

3 drops Chamomile

3 drops Clary Sage

3 drops Geranium

6 drops Lavender

1 tablespoon cider vinegar

2 ounces witch hazel

5 ounces water

Mix ingredients together and use in onr or both of the following ways:

- As a toner after you cleanse your skin, before you apply moisturizer.

- You can also use this to tone the bikini area after you shave.

PLAY IT AGAIN, SAM

As you already may have noticed, many remedies are good for more than one thing. The toner recipe above is also good for shave burn as well as avoiding those red dots you get after shaving or depilitating the bikini area.

REST EASY BODY RUB

Sometimes, you just need a little pampering escape. The following body rub is really best when you can have someone else massage you with it. But self-application (second best, we know) works well too.

Once you apply Relaxing Body Rub, it's generally best to go to bed or at least lie down. Don't try to operate any machinery or help anyone with math homework.

RELAXING BODY RUB

6 drops Cedar

3 drops Clary Sage

6 drops Orange

Mix the oils and use in any of the following ways:

↪ Combine the essential oils with 2 ounces canola oil in a pretty bottle. Use this as a body rub to really relax you before bedtime.

↪ Add the essential oil blend to 2 tablespoons petroleum jelly and rub a little on your pulse points (wrist and temples) before bedtime.

GET IT WET

This blend is also great used in a bath or a diffuser.

Guess what I like when I am getting a relaxing massage or enjoying a calm bath? That's right, candles and soothing music are in the background, giving me a wonderful experience for all my senses.

—Judi

TIME TO ESCAPE

Clary Sage is great help during the challenges of April—did we mention taxes? Once you've taken care of your "To Do" list, reward yourself—and your partner—with a relaxing blend used in a romantic massage.

Especially for You

Passion's sweetness reigns
Over evening's life and breath
Jasmine rules the night

Once you experience the heavenly scent of Jasmine, you will understand why they call it "the Queen of the Night" in India. And you will never forget her.

The flower of a tree of the sweet olive family provides Jasmine's essence. Picked before sunrise, grown in warm exotic countries like Morocco, China, and India, Jasmine is rare and costly. Jasmine's deep sweetness enhances love, sex, and sleep. It is said that Jasmine gives your nighttime dreams a new dimension. Use Jasmine to raise your spirits, relax your body, and open yourself to love. Try the following massage oil with your loved one for a time of relaxed pleasure.

OPEN LOVING MASSAGE

2 drops Jasmine, 2 drops Orange, 4 drops Cedar, 1 drop Ylang Ylang. Add the essential oils to 1 ounce of canola oil and mix well. Take lots of time with your massage.

ROMANTIC ESCAPE MASSAGE

2 drops Cedar

2 drops Clary Sage

1 drop Orange

2 drops pure vanilla extract

2 ounces canola oil

Combine all these ingredients and slowly massage into your partner's skin. Take your time. Give extra attention to all those tight and stressed spots.

🌣 The way to health is to take an aromatic bath and scented massage every day.

—Hippocrates

BANISH THAT BAD MOOD

Often you know just what is causing a bad mood and to improve your mood, you can work on the problem. Sometimes, you just feel bad or mad or simply not nice. We used to try to analyze it. Now, we just admit to having a case of the "megrims" and use an essential oil to help it pass. Often, Clary Sage comes to mind first.

Using the recipe below with a nice cup of tea and a few quiet minutes works wonders on the megrims.

🌣 There is no such thing as a crash course in serenity.

—Shirley Maclaine

---— ✌ ✍ ——---

RECIPE FOR BAD MOOD CURE

1 drop Clary Sage

Drop the oil onto a tissue or cotton ball and inhale, or add the oil to hot water to diffuse into the air. Take ten and inhale the aroma. Almost magically, your mood will lift.

🍀 *At this time of the year, my bad moods usually seem to be related to tax preparation; I'm sure you can relate.*

NAIL CARE

Even though we are only planning our gardens now, our nails seem to know that very soon they will be abused by digging in dirt. The following blend is especially good for dry cuticles, but your nails and hands will enjoy the special treatment too.

---— ✌ ✍ ——---

RECIPE FOR CUTICLE CARE TREATMENT

4 drops Clary Sage

2 drops Geranium

4 drops Lavender

2 drops Rosemary

Mix the essential oils into 1 tablespoon sweet almond oil and ½ teaspoon castor oil.

Rub this mixture into your nails and up into the cuticles before bed nightly.

Use this treatment for 30 days and you will notice a great improvement.

🍀 *This is a great year-round blend to keep your nails strong and healthy.*

—Judi

DON'T CRAMP MY STYLE

Women don't have the market on cramps, although it may seem that way each month. But we can all be attacked by cramps due to muscle strain or overindulgence. Don't let cramps cramp your style.

--- ✣ ---

RECIPE FOR CRAMP RELIEVER

4 drops Clary Sage

2 drops Fennel

2 drops Geranium

Mix the essential oils into 1 tablespoon base oil and massage stomach area gently.

AIR SPRAY

Sometimes you can use Clary Sage to energize. In the recipe below, it serves to lighten your mood, probably from the feeling it gives you of lightening your load.

Especially for You

To some of us, Jasmine is irresistible as a perfume. Just a drop on your wrists and neck (and perhaps on some of your more intimate places) envelops you in the sensuality of the East. But you also might like to personalize a perfume for yourself. Because Jasmine is expensive, always mix the smallest amount possible to determine if you like the scent. You can't feel sexy for others if you don't like how you smell. Also, when blending Jasmine with other ingredients, add the least expensive ingredients first. That way, if it's really not working, you can decide *before* you add your precious Jasmine. Try this one to begin.

ROAD TO SHANGRI-LA

Mix 3 drops Jasmine, 1 drop Sandalwood, and 1 drop Clary Sage together. Apply the tiniest bit to your pulse points. This combination will leave a lasting impression on those who come close to you.

RECIPE FOR ENERGIZING

5 drops Clary Sage

15 drops Lavender

10 drops Lemon

16 ounces water

Combine the essential oils with water in a spray bottle. Spray this into the air in a room for a sweet, slightly energizing spray.

🌿 *This blend is a must whenever I travel. After a long flight or a long day of meetings, I treat myself to a rejuvenating spray.*

—Judi

Calming with Clary Sage

When you think of Clary Sage think of relaxing, whether you need to relax aging skin, relieve anxiety or fear, or just soothe your weary bones.

Sometimes Easter is in April and sometimes it is not. But one constant of April is the 15th—that red-letter day when we are scrambling around to make sure our taxes are post-marked with that date. So indulge yourself with Clary Sage during this stressful time. I make up the following potpourri when I am going buggy-eyed over a calculator and more IRS forms than I know what to do with. Try it!

🌿 *When I think of Clary Sage I think of blends that relax me and blends that put me in a sensual mood. The combination of feelings is very special.*

—Judi

CALM AND CONCENTRATE

5 drops Clary Sage

Lemon rinds

Apple peels

16 ounces water

Mix the rinds and peels into the water in a potpourri pot or saucepan. Add the Clary Sage and warm. You'll love how you are able to remain calm and focused.

🐦 Adventure is worthwhile in itself.

—*Amelia Earhart*

If you like Clary Sage, you might also like Sandalwood for its relaxing, musky-smelling benefits. Sandalwood is a luxurious scent often used in exotic perfumes. It has a lower, relaxing tone and calms and relaxes you.

Geranium

Pelargonium graveolens

The year's at the spring and day's at the morn;
Morning's at seven; The hillside's dew-pearled;
The lark's on the wing: The snail's on the thorn;
God's in His heaven—All's right with the world.
—*Robert Browning*

get out the running shoes

hmmm, lilacs

I love being a mother

May flowers

lovely sound, birds singing

new breath of life

spirits awaken

sun dries my waterlogged thoughts

Celebration!

May also honors mothers. The arrival of my daughter late in my life has given me an appreciation of the role and responsibilities we have to our children, to all the children of the world, to other parents, and to ourselves. Let's use May to honor these goals.

—Judi

May celebrates life in so many ways. It honors us with the beauty of flowers—their radiance, freshness, and new growth remind us to strive for the same in ourselves. Its new-found warmth encourages us to look with warmth and love at our hibernated wintry thoughts. Its life-giving rain teaches us to shake off the showers of life's trials and appreciate the new blossoms of life's joys.

May is a rejuvenating month. The frigid grounds of winter finally give way to plants and flowers that offer fragrance, color, and the hopeful perspective of rebirth.

Geranium is a terrific oil for this month. It symbolizes all that May reflects; new growth, nurturing, and hope. It is an important oil in just about every blend that deals with skin and hair care. It is also attuned to female concerns with its balancing influence on hormonal conditions. And it also promotes a sense of well-being and self-worth during all stages of life. So join us now as we celebrate Geranium and how it celebrates life.

Geranium

Geranium is a favored partner of other essential oils because it adapts its various properties to blend effectively. Its floral fragrance, which makes it a pleasure to use either on its own or with other oils, also adapts to the blend in which it is used, mimicking other scents in an unusual and enhancing way.

There are over 300 varieties of Geranium that vary in scent depending on where they are grown. Geranium is a favorite of many who use aromatherapy because of its positive impact in the treatment of both medical conditions and emotional concerns. It soothes the spirit as it lavishes mental comfort and offers potent healing assistance to your body.

There are three areas in which Geranium excels: skin and hair care, as an emotional balancer and uplifter, and in regulating hormonal balance. We have included blends that show off Geranium's shining properties. In addition, its antiseptic and astringent properties enhance its overall usefulness in the treatment of many conditions, including cuts, burns, and wounds.

May's sunshine, warm breezes, and refreshing light rains promote the development and well-being of all that grows in this month. Geranium has its own sunshine that helps rejuvenate skin cells, promoting a vibrant glow. May's warm breezes are found in Geranium's characteristics that promote a fresh, harmonious, and quieting balance on an emotional level. And the refreshing light rain of Geranium's impact on hormones revitalizes us and promotes a feeling of overall well-being.

Remedies

Highlighting Geranium's impressive skin-care properties, we offer blends that touch the most sensitive skin of our children's diaper areas, our big boys' sensitive facial skin, and all types of skin bothered by harsh weather, poison ivy, or normal living conditions.

Every cause and form of stress is positively influenced by Geranium, and we offer blends for headaches and relaxation. Many recipes for hormonal balancing, general healing, and anxiety reduction include Geranium because of its combined medicinal and emotional benefits.

And finally, we celebrate women by offering some suggestions of how Geranium can meet some of our personal needs in terms of menstrual issues.

Note: Geranium's fragrance is very powerful, and may be overwhelming to some people. Before you shelve it, remember that its smell adjusts to other oils it is combined with, so experiment to find an appealing scent. Remember also that it is not the aroma of the oil that makes it so effective medicinally. A great scent is a wonderful side benefit.

❦ I started my journey into the wonderful world of aromatherapy as a natural way to treat my newborn. Little did I know then the myriad of ways aromatherapy was going to positively influence not only her life, but those of all the important people in my life.

—Judi

PAMPERING BODY PARTS

Geranium works extremely well with Chamomile and creates rich blends that soothe skin conditions. In addition, the sparkling effects these blends have on your skin reflect the way you feel inside. The following blend is especially effective for your infant's tender tushy, and is great wherever skin rash appears.

RECIPE FOR DIAPER RASH TREATMENT

1 drop Chamomile

3 drops Geranium

2 drops Lavender

Clean the diaper area with warm water to which you have added a drop of Chamomile. Use a soft all-cotton towel or cloth.

Mix oils together. You can use this blend in any of the following ways:

- Add to 2 tablespoons almond oil and massage baby's diaper area to reduce diaper rash.

- Use 1 drop of blend in a pleasant bath.

- For a persistent diaper rash, combine this blend with water instead of the base oil, spritz the child's diaper area, and then sprinkle on cornstarch.

If diaper rash has caused your child to be fretful and uncomfortable, you can make a double batch of this blend and use it to give your child a relaxing and soothing massage. Don't forget to use firm but gentle strokes, and make the experience even more memorable with a calming lullaby.

Worry is the misuse of imagination.

—*Audrey Woodhall*

I grew up in New England and thought it was the only area that experienced rapid change in weather. I now live in the Southeast and find that a cool morning breeze, heat and humidity, and a sultry night can all exist in just one day.

—Judi

Add Orange to the recipe above for a fun bath for children of all ages.

Our skin is put through so many trials and tribulations in a normal day, especially if you live where the elements can change without a moment's notice. Let aromatherapy help guard your skin and help create a pleasing and attractive appearance.

The following shave blend was originally created for men as a shaving spray, but for all of you women who also spend a great deal of time attached to a razor, try it. The essential oils in this treatment make it gentle enough to use every day, and safe enough to use on even the most intimate shaving areas.

RECIPE FOR RAZOR BURN RELIEF

3 drops Chamomile

5 drops Geranium

5 drops Lavender

3 drops Lemon

Mix all oils together.

↬ Put half the blend into a quart of water and spritz the shaved area.

↬ For a more concentrated effect, put the other half of the blend into 2 tablespoons of vegetable oil and massage the shaved area.

This blend also has a wonderful light fragrance that is pleasing and uplifting.

START CLEAN, SHAVE SMOOTHLY

A friend suggests that you clean the area to be shaved with a Provodine-Iodine solution (sold over-the-counter in pharmacies). This reduces the spread of germs, cleanses the area thoroughly, and reduces inflammation and those annoying little red dots.

This blend has also been very effective in the treatment of chapped skin, so make up a batch for year-round use. Putting a small container in with your ski or skating equipment makes it readily available after a day of frigid fun.

As you can see, Geranium consistently appears in recipes that deal with all types of skin care. Keep a bottle of Geranium with your beauty supplies and hair care products as a reliable partner in your fight for healthy skin and hair.

Give a container to your child for use after sports activities. It is never too early to start children on their way to understanding the need to protect themselves and keep an eye on their health.

For everyday use, whether it be after your bath, to focus on those extra-dry knees, elbows, and heels, or to soothe a case of dry, flaky skin, the next recipe is a big hit.

RECIPE FOR SKIN SOOTHER

10 drops Chamomile

10 drops Geranium

10 drops Lavender

Blend oils together.

- Use 6 drops of the blend in 2 teaspoons of aloe vera gel to relieve chapped lips.

- Put 8 drops of the blend in 2 tablespoons of vegetable oil for an after-bath massage, or to focus on the extra dry and flaky skin areas.

- Put 8 drops into a pint of water and use as a toner for your face and body. This is ideal for all skin types.

- Add a few drops of the blend to your favorite hand cream to make it more effective in treating the symptoms of dry, damaged skin on hands.

STOP SCRATCHING

Add a drop of Eucalyptus and Tea Tree Oil to this blend to help treat prickly heat, poison ivy, and similar skin irritations.

You are unique, and if that is not fulfilled, then something wonderful has been lost.

—*Martha Graham*

Especially for You

Tropical love isle
Hear waterfalls, feel the sun
Paradise at home

Ylang-Ylang is a passionate oil that is often used in perfumes. While its scent may be attractive to the person who smells the oil, for the person who wears it, Ylang-Ylang is also a proven physical and psychological stress-reliever. Its sweet, heady, floral fragrance is the best of both the scent and healing worlds. The essential oil of Ylang-Ylang is produced from the flower of a tropical tree, the Cananga odorata, which grows in such exotic places as Zanzibar, Haiti, and Hawaii. As with some other essential oils derived from flowers, Ylang-Ylang blossoms must be harvested before sunrise to preserve the precious oils.

SEXY AND SOOTHING

Put 5 drops of Ylang-Ylang, 4 drops of Patchouli, and 6 drops of Orange anywhere (well, anywhere external). It's great in a bath or a diffuser, or as a massage oil to make you and your partner feel sexy and soothed.

S-T-R-E-S-S (NEED WE SAY MORE?)

So much research has been done about stress—what causes it, what are its symptoms, how to treat and prevent it. Who-ever identifies a surefire method for treating stress will be the next century's Nobel Prize winner. But until that dis-covery, let us suggest some natural solutions: relaxation, meditation, visualization, and massage.

Treating the cause of stress is obviously the key to suc-cess, but often that quest is a lifetime journey for peace and tranquility. The following blend helps give you a sneak pre-view of that frame of mind, or at least serves as an oasis of stress relief. Relax and enjoy!

RECIPE FOR STRESS RELIEF

10 drops Chamomile

5 drops Geranium

10 drops Lavender

5 drops Lemon

Mix oils together.

- Put 8 drops of the blend into a soothing bath or sauna.

- The same blend applied to the temples, back of the neck, across the forehead, and behind the ears is a wonderful relief for stress-induced headaches.

Geranium is an oil that adapts very well and contributes to other oils; that is why Geranium is a very effective oil in the treatment of all types of stress. Whether the stress has been caused by emotional situations, work-related issues, family, finances—the list goes on and on—Geranium is a dependable ally.

FINDING BALANCE

You can't pick up a women's magazine without reading an article about menstruation, hormonal imbalance, infertility, menopause, or some other intimate aspect of women's biology. For hundreds of years, women have had to deal with these issues, yet they continue to be as current a concern as they have always been.

It seems that moving into the twenty-first century will only include more factors that can alter the delicate balance we strive to find in our lives. Geranium can come to the rescue. Its strong medicinal properties treat the body while the soothing and uplifting emotional characteristics treat the mind.

The following blend is the basic balance foundation for just about every blend that deals with hormonal issues, from first-time menstrual cramps to the confusion and varied effects of menopause. It is also suitable for treating extremely heavy bleeding.

BASIC BALANCE BLEND

10 drops Chamomile

10 drops Geranium

10 drops Lavender

Mix oils together.

Add the oils to 2 tablespoons of a desired base oil (vegetable oil is fine), and massage in a V pattern up from the vaginal area, over the lower abdomen and hips, back toward the buttocks, and end the V above the anus.

ADDING TO THE BASICS

The following table shows you how to add to this Basic Balance blend to treat specialized feminine concerns:

ADD	TO TREAT	USAGE
5 drops Orange 5 drops Lemon	Low self-esteem, anxiety, or tension associated with your period or pregnancy.	Massage as directed above, or place 8 drops into a soothing bath.
2 drops Fennel 2 drops Clary Sage	General and postnatal hormonal imbalance.	Massage as directed above, or place 8 drops into a soothing bath
3 drops Clary Sage	Symptoms of PMS, including irritability or listlessness.	Massage as directed above, or place 8 drops into a soothing bath

AND THERE'S MORE!

Geranium's antiseptic and astringent properties make it a key oil for general care. Here is a blend that can be used for everyday first-aid:

––––––––––––––– ⅏ ⅏ –––––––––––––––

RECIPE TO USE FOR CUTS AND WOUNDS

Chamomile

Geranium

Lavender

These oils are effective in cleaning and healing cuts and wounds. Use Lavender and Chamomile to clean the wound and use Geranium to promote the rejuvenation of skin cells.

- Put 1 drop of each oil in 2 teaspoons of witch hazel and 1 tablespoon icewater for the treatment of black eyes or other facial bruises.

- Add a drop of Rosemary to these oils and use both hot and cold compresses to treat bruises and swelling.

- These oils have also been recognized as relievers of hay fever symptoms. Put 1 drop of each oil into 1 teaspoon vegetable oil and massage the neck and chest areas.

🌷 The human heart, at whatever age, opens to the heart that opens in return.

—*Marie Edgeworth*

Especially for You

Because Ylang-Ylang mixes well with so many oils in this book, we encourage you to experiment to find the physically, psychologically, and emotionally soothing blend that is just right for you. Ylang-Ylang blends well with Sandalwood, Jasmine, Rosewood, Bergamot, Rose, and Patchouli.

SET THE STAGE

Put one drop of Ylang-Ylang and one drop of another essential oil of your choice on your pillowcase. That will help put you and your partner in the right frame of mind for pillow-talk.

Incorporating More Gernanium into Your Life

Because of its calming effects, Geranium is great in baths. Settle children down while soothing their skin, or allow yourself to relax your cares away and enhance the condition of your skin at the same time.

Put a potpourri arrangement that contains Geranium in your dressing room or bathroom; it's a great way to start the day. You can grow geranium plants of many different scents. Rose, mint, and lemon are a few of the scented geraniums available. Interestingly enough, the scent is in the leaves of these plants. You can use them in herbal tea or in potpourris.

If you like the flowery aroma of Geranium, you might also like the flowery aroma of Ylang-Ylang, our bonus oil for this month. It's sweet, comfortable scent smells like sun-warmed flowers in the Caribbean.

Long-term change requires looking honestly at our lives and realizing that it's nice to be needed, but not at the expense of our health, happiness, and sanity.

—*Ellen Sue Stern*

OIL OF THE MONTH

Chamomile

Chamaemelum nobile

It is the month of June,

The month of leaves and roses,

When pleasant sights

salute the eyes,

and pleasant scents the noses.

—*Nathaniel P. Willis*

school's out for the summer!

these first really hot days feel great

shorts and sneakers everywhere

weddings

smell the flowers

hiking through the mountains

sunglasses

sun warms you to the bone—finally

lollipops

lazy afternoons at the lake

water-dappled sun escapes your fingertips

Summertime, and the Living is Easy

Isn't it strange that what took so long and seemed so difficult in the midst of winter is now almost effortless? Going to the store? Load the kids into the car, don't worry about sweaters and umbrellas. Time to eat? Make a salad and have some fruit. Kids with Popsicles melted down their arms? Wash them off with the hose or dip them in the pond.

Summer officially begins this month and school lets out, giving a definite vacation feeling to the air, even if you don't get your actual vacation for several more weeks. And really—when do parents ever have a vacation?

But before summer begins, June offers us emotional events in the form of weddings and graduations. The calming properties of Chamomile, our featured oil, can really help, along with a box of tissues, as we watch loved ones enter a new phase of their lives.

Even summer, with its warmth and ease, keeps you on guard. Stinging bugs and itchy bites are on vacation too, making a buffet of your skin. Or maybe it's a job for them as they leave their calling cards of bumps and itches. And we can't forget that we need to be careful of those wonderful rays of sun. Too much of a good thing can cause pain and damage; Chamomile can help.

Chamomile is a good oil for the beginning of summer. It's gentle and calming, good for happy times, and will help ease you into summer.

🌸 Be glad of life because it gives you the chance to love, to work, to play, and to look up at the stars . . . .

—*Henry Van Dyke*

Chamomile

Chamomile comes from a flowering plant that is a member of the sunflower family. Chamomile is, in fact, a yellow flower almost daisy-like in appearance. It's usually grown in eastern and southern Europe.

There are two popular types of Chamomile: German and Roman. Roman Chamomile oil is a yellow-green color, speaking of the promises of new growth and healing. German Chamomile oil is a cool, deep blue color because of its high azulene content. Some facial preparations use azulene as a key ingredient because of its skin-soothing properties. Chamomile's strength is in soothing skin.

The Roman Chamomile oil used in this book is antibacterial, antiseptic, and disinfectant, but it is most valued for its anti-inflammatory properties, whether infection, a bug bite, or sunburn causes inflammation. Chamomile is useful in treating burns, rashes, and fevers.

Chamomile is also a sedative oil with stress-relieving properties—from the head of the plant to your head.

It's very good at treating the megrims, those bad, anxious, crabby feelings that don't always have a specific origin. We used to analyze why we might be feeling that way. Now, soothing the feeling away is the quicker, better solution. Chamomile has analgesic, sedative, and calming properties. Many herbal tea preparations for sleeplessness have Chamomile as a main ingredient.

🌱 Joy is what happens to us when we allow ourselves to recognize how good things really are.

—*Marianne Williamson*

The gentle properties of Chamomile make it perfect for children when they are irritable, unable to sleep, or experiencing other normal aches and pains of childhood like teething and tummy-aches.

Remedies

In this chapter, you will find Chamomile-based remedies for irritable babies, irritable skin, and just plain irritable people; real help for weather-dried skin, headaches, sleepless children, colicky children, and sleepless parents. You'll also discover some aromatic ways to use Chamomile as a pre-bedtime air spray, both for little folk and bigger folk.

Chamomile, with its calming and soothing properties, is perfect to quiet skin, emotions, and those high energy levels of early summer. It's so soothing that it works extremely well with Lavender directly on the skin for burns, or diluted in a water-based spray for sunburn.

Our young ones know (or soon learn) that Chamomile goes with some of the bad (and some not-so-bad things) of life, such as boo-boos, bug bites, and bedtime. Chamomile is probably the second most-frequently used essential oil in treating insect bites and bee stings. Lavender is first with its antitoxin effect, but you want to follow that up with the pain-alleviating qualities of Chamomile. Both oils, of course, are valuable in dealing with insect insults because of their antiseptic qualities.

Gardeners, like plants, invariably grow from small beginnings.

—*Geraldine Holt*

KIDS' STUFF

Chamomile is one of the essential oils that is safe for children of all ages, from newborns to tots to teens. In this section, we are going to give you a few recipes to cover the hurts that bother babies and toddlers.

Colic and teething can be as aggravating to parents as they are to a child. These two discomforts are often bewildering to parents because the cause is not always obvious. Chamomile can help. Think of the worst gas pains you ever had and handle that colicky baby's belly accordingly.

RECIPE FOR COLIC CURE

1 drop Chamomile

1 teaspoon olive oil

Put one drop of Chamomile essential oil in your palm. Pour about 1 teaspoon of olive oil into your palm. Rub your palms together, warming the oil mixture and spreading it around your palms. Gently rub some of this on your baby's belly. Don't rush. Cover the baby's belly with an undershirt or a soft blanket to keep in the warmth.

It seems that once a baby grows out of the colicky age, it's time to start teething. With teething, you must acquire experience to recognize the signs quickly. Once you've been

We know enough of the internal workings of the seed to stand in awe at its variety, its toughness, and its practical simplicity.

—Nancy Bubel

This is a great recipe for fretfulness. Between the gentle massage and a lullaby, your little one will drift off to sleep.

—Judi

🌿 *I also used one drop of Chamomile mixed in 2 tablespoons of cold water. Then I would stick my finger in the blend and rub it on Chelsea's gum.*

—Judi

through teething (your child's teething, that is, thank goodness you've forgotten your own!) you quickly recognize the flushed cheeks, drooling, and irritability for what it is—just another tooth on its way. While this is a comfort to know, you and your child still need relief. The remedy for teething pain is as simple as the colic remedy.

TEETHING SOLUTION

5 drops Chamomile

2 ounces Aloe Vera

Mix the two ingredients and use this to massage the outside of the jaw. If you keep the mixture cool, it also counteracts the heat of the teething process.

Remember what it felt like when your wisdom teeth came in? And you only had four of those. Teething Solution would have probably been a good remedy.

EMERGENCY BURN OINTMENT

Chamomile is a great anti-inflammatory. It works well for any kind of inflammation, from an infected scratch to a feverish brow.

Obviously, if you see no improvement or if the burn is a serious one, take yourself and the burn to the emergency room.

———————— ⚬⚬ ————————

RECIPE FOR BURN MIRACLE

3 drops Chamomile

3 drops Peppermint

Palmful of hand cream

You could probably use any kind of hand cream, vegetable oil, or (since this is an emergency) water or milk. A palmful is approximately one tablespoon.

Mix it all together and apply it to the burn often.

QUIT BUGGING ME!

As soon as the weather gets warm, the bugs get going. And each bug seems to have its favorite month; May flies, June bugs, mosquitoes in July.

Some oils, like Lavender (July) and Peppermint (August), are very good at repelling bugs; but Chamomile is very good at alleviating the pain and itch of bites when you do get them.

BUG BITE RELIEF

Chamomile is one of the essential oils you can apply directly to your skin; it's that gentle. Yet it works powerfully.

One day at work I accidentally put my hand into a stream of boiling water. Although Lavender was always my oil of choice for any kind of burn, I was Lavenderless at that moment. The following recipe worked like a miracle. The pain went away almost immediately and the redness was minimal. My fingers never even peeled.
—Paula

This blend also works well on itchy skin. The Peppermint takes care of the itch, while Chamomile soothes the skin. I use it when those little critters start feasting on my skin or on my dog.
—Judi

Bugs also have their favorite people and I seem to be one of them!
—Paula

Apply a drop of Chamomile to a bite. You'll notice the change in itchiness and excess warmth in minutes.

CHANGES IN TEMPERATURE

As the seasons change, so does your skin. June, the month that transitions us from cool, tentative spring to hot and active summer, points out your skin's changing needs like no other month until fall is upon us.

———————————— ✂ ✄ ————————————

RECIPE FOR COOLING TONER

3 drops Chamomile

3 drops Clary Sage

3 drops Geranium

6 drops Lavender

1 tablespoon cider vinegar

2 ounces witch hazel

Mix the essential oils together with the vinegar and witch hazel in an 8-ounce bottle. Add enough distilled water to fill the bottle.

Use this toner in the morning and at night before you moisturize.

TO SLEEP, PERCHANCE TO DREAM

June days can be absolutely exhilarating. There's so much to do inside and out, at school and at home. There's never enough time in the day for all that cleaning and gardening, sports, and just going for an evening walk. And even though your body may be tired at the end of the day, sometimes your mind just won't turn off. Chamomile can help.

Added to milk or bath oil, Chamomile makes a relaxing bath. You can also try Chamomile blended with other essential oils. Try a leisurely soak before you end your busy day.

— ❧ ☙ —

RELAXING BATH

2 drops Cedar

2 drops Chamomile

2 drops Geranium

1 drop Lemon

2 ounces hazelnut oil or milk

Mix the essential oils into the oil or milk. Use the hazelnut oil if your skin is suffering from residual effects of a long, cold, windy winter. Use the milk for some soothing relief from your June activities.

Pour this into a tub of warm water and relax for 20 minutes.

❦ Whenever I take a relaxing bath, I find that candles and soft music add to the overall feeling of relaxation. I can transport myself to a quiet, gentle place where the troubles of the day melt away.

—Judi

Especially for You

Brides, grooms, and weddings
Last-minute details gone wrong
Enjoy peaceful calm

Neroli, better known as Orange Blossom or Orange Flower, represents joy and sensuality. It also eases anxiety and makes you feel peaceful—a perfect combination for brides or others in romantic situations.

This essential oil is named after the seventeenth-century Princess of Nerole. The scent of this floral oil recalls its Sicilian homeland, rich and warm and dreamy. This is probably the most expensive floral oil. The blooms must be picked by hand and it takes over 1,000 pounds of orange blossoms to make one pound of essential oil. Use the following blend to help you calm down and get in the mood for love.

HONEYMOON NIGHTS

2 drops of Neroli, 2 drops of Rose, and 4 drops of Rosewood. Place in a bath, diffuser, or lamp ring.

If the keyed-up person who probably won't sleep easily tonight is your child, and your child is dreading bedtime (can you imagine dreading bedtime?), add the following to their tub.

KIDS' BATH

1 drop Chamomile

2 drops Lavender

1 drop Orange

Mix the oils together and add them to tepid water for your child's pre-bedtime bath.

You can also use the Kids' Bath blend in an air spray, but increase the amounts as in the following recipe for Kids' Bedtime Spray.

BEDTIME SPRAY

A bedtime spray works well for many reasons, the first being the therapeutic value of the essential oils. The other reasons have more to do with being a child: bedtime is scary and under someone else's control. The problem with bedtime could start with the change of seasons, the switch to or from Daylight Savings Time, a move to a new house, or just a

We often make up a name for the spray. Names have varied from "Monster Spray" to "Relaxing Spray."

—Paula

change in routine. Let your child help make the spray,
smelling and approving each essential oil before you add it to
the spray container.

Let your child pick out a colorful spray container. Label
it with the name they picked. Let your child spray their
room before going to bed.

————————————— ✂ 🎀 —————————————

RECIPE FOR KIDS' BEDTIME SPRAY

12 drops Chamomile

12 drops Lavender

8 drops Orange

Mix the oils together with 16 ounces of water. Use this to
spray the air and pillow in the room of the soon-to-be
sweet dreamer.

SWEET DREAM MIX

3 drops Chamomile

3 drops Orange

5 ounces water

Mix ingredients in a small spray container.

Spray pillows, sheets, windows, and anywhere monsters
lurk.

Children usually enjoy spraying this themselves. Some favorite places are under the bed and in the closet.

Two-ounce hair spray containers are perfect for small hands. A label with fun drawings or stickers makes it more special.

Adults have monsters too, but they usually look more like over-scheduled days, budgets that won't balance, or bosses that aren't very communicative. Whatever the reason, there will be some times you'll need a "monster spray" of your own.

The bedtime sprays can be used for children of all ages, even teens. Just don't tell them!

❧ *Last year I had a nervous house guest, AJ, an eight-year-old boy with a very active imagination which did not turn off at bedtime. He thought about monsters a lot. You know, the kind that lurk behind closet doors, around corners, and under the bed? I'm much older than AJ and I still don't hang my arms over the side of the bed at night. So I made some Sweet Dream Mix, which AJ and I used to spray every place in his room (in the closet, too) and his pillow every night before bedtime. And AJ started sleeping very well.*

—Paula

Keeping Calm with Chamomile

You might also want to invest in some herbal teas which include Chamomile or a delicious blend of Chamomile and other herbs. These can help relax you, calm your stomach, or help you sleep. A cooled Chamomile tea also makes a nice spray for hot or itchy skin.

Chamomile is a great herb to add to potpourri because it has such a nice look, and it mixes well with other herbs to

Especially for You

Neroli is wonderful for all types of skin, including sensitive skin, so feel free to massage to your body's content. Use Neroli sparingly because just a touch of its sweetness will have long-lasting, memorable results.

NUPTIAL NEROLI NECTAR

Put 2 drops of Clary Sage, 2 drops of Cedar, 2 drops of Bergamot, and 2 drops of Neroli into 2 tablespoons of vegetable oil, and let the massage begin.

make a delightful blend that pleases your senses. Chamomile is probably the most advertised of all of the essential oils. You can find Chamomile commercially used in teas, potpourri, stomach remedies, heating pads, beauty products, and more.

If you like Chamomile, you might also like Calendula, an oil made from marigolds. It's harder to find and more expensive than Chamomile, but extremely good for skin. You might also make use of Calendula in a premixed skin ointment.

One year, I made a bookmark (lace for the women, cloth for the men) for each member of my family who loves to read. To it I added a drop of Chamomile. Now, I am no arts and crafts person, but these gifts got rave reviews. I think the essential oil helped.

—Judi

OIL OF THE MONTH

Lavender

Lavandula angustifolia or *L. x intermedia*

Here's your sweet Lavender,
sixteen sprigs a penny,
Which you'll find, my ladies,
will smell as sweet as any.
—*traditional cry of London flower vendors*

lighter later

independence and all its freedom

no regular dinnertime

let's have ice cream instead

softball

hot dogs and burgers

cookouts

hot days at the beach

poison ivy

afternoons at the pool

sun, sun, sun

This Is the Summer You Dreamed About

It's July, and baby, it's hot outside! The summer vacation you were fantasizing about during those winter storms is finally here. And with it, all the fun that summer brings: picnics, days at the beach, gardening—you get the picture.

Of course there is the flip side to the fun of July—sunburn, bug bites, and poison ivy, which can make you feel like one big itch. You might call these the challenges of July. Fortunately, aromatherapy gives you solutions to the hazards of this month.

One of the best oils for July's challenges is Lavender. Its cooling and soothing qualities can keep you from scratching your way through the month, a less-than-gracious picture, you must admit.

Lavender leaves us gliding coolly through the summer (think of Daisy Buchanan dressed in gauzy white linen dresses in her beachside mansion). There's also something old-fashioned about the smell, reminiscent of stored linens in those wonderful and mysterious steamer trunks lucky people have in their attic.

Lavender

Lavender comes from the beautiful bluish-purple flowers of the Lavender plant. The fragrance of the oil is fresh and sharp with a hint of rain-washed trees. Its scent is more sporty than flowery.

Lavender is extracted from the freshly-cut flowering tops of the plant harvested during the months of July and August. The harvesting is done during the hottest time of the day because that is when the essential oil content of the plant is at its highest.

One of the interesting things you learn in the study of aromatherapy is that the plant itself gives you clues about its strengths. Oils from flowers are often good for skin-related conditions and emotions; Lavender is no exception.

Lavender oil is a natural antibiotic, antiseptic, and detoxifier that prevents infection and promotes healing. These antiseptic and antibacterial properties make it useful to treat infections and deal with bacterial conditions. The detoxifying properties also make Lavender helpful with sunburn, insect bites, and allergic skin rashes.

The name Lavender comes from the Latin word *lavare,* which means "to wash." It is cleansing and deodorizing, and on a more emotional level, stimulating, calming, and refreshing. Strange that it could be both stimulating and calming, but Lavender is one of the essential oils that is an adaptogen, meaning its properties adapt to your needs. Kind of a nice concept, don't you think?

The calming properties of Lavender make it a natural sedative. It's also great to use for children because it is so gentle.

Lavender is one of the most versatile essential oils around. With its cooling and soothing properties, Lavender may soon become your closest summer companion.

Remedies

In this chapter, you will find Lavender-based remedies for burns, sunburn, dry peeling skin, bug bites, poison oak and ivy, and the occasional sleeplessness of summer, as well as insect repellent (get them before they get you). You'll also discover some aromatic ways to use Lavender as a disinfectant—it is much nicer smelling, less toxic, and less expensivethan store-bought aerosol.

You can apply Lavender directly to the skin; it's good for burns, scratches, and bug bites. Dab a little Lavender onto a blemish to use its antibiotic effect to fight infection and its cooling effect to relieve the itch at the same time.

Our young ones know that Lavender usually goes on little boo-boos right after Mom's kiss. We recommend both. You can also use Lavender in water-based sprays, as you will see in the recipes in this chapter.

COUNTER CLEANER

A few drops of Lavender in a water spray make a pleasant and mild disinfectant for countertops. For stronger action, add a few drops of Eucalyptus.

Lavender also works well in a vegetable oil base (such as sweet almond, canola, or olive oil) for a skin rub or massage. Diluted in milk or bath oil, it makes a relaxing bath. You can

🌿 Shall I compare thee to a
  summer's day?
Thou art more lovely and more
  temperate:
Rough winds do shake the
  darling buds of May,
and summer's lease hath all too
  short a date . . . .
  —*Shakespeare*

Especially for You

Sweetness, borne of wood
Disguised floral, so lovely
Flies on wings of dreams

Rosewood lends some mystery to the bright, sun-laden month of July. Its sweet, floral, woody fragrance is such an unusual combination of flowers and trees. Sometimes called Bois de Rose, it is produced in Brazil from the wood of the Aniba roseadora tree, a member of the Laurel family. This essential oil is calming, helps relieve tiredness, and lifts your mood. Lavender, the other oil introduced this month, combines well with Rosewood for a relaxing and refreshing aroma. As you try out Rosewood with other oils, keep in mind that while it is flowery and spicy it is also a wood, and very relaxing.

Let the object of your affection smell your hair after you start using this hair conditioner, which is good for strengthening dry hair.

SWEET HAIR CONDITIONER

Eight drops Rosewood, 8 drops Cedar, 8 drops Rosemary. Add the essential oils to 8 ounces of an unscented hair conditioner. Apply to your hair after you shampoo and let it sit 5 minutes before you rinse it out.

🌸 The earth laughs in flowers.
—*Ralph Waldo Emerson*

also try Lavender, in combination with other essential oils, in cornstarch as a talcum powder substitute.

FINE WASHABLES

Use Lavender in rinse water when you do hand-washables.

Warning: Never put Lavender (or any essential oil) in your eyes. And always wash your hands after working with essential oils so you don't accidentally rub some into your eyes.

THE OUCHES OF SUMMER

Now that the weather is comfortable enough for you to go out with very little clothing on, you probably seem to notice more of the local wildlife—bugs! There are crawling bugs, flying bugs, and bugs that just seem to show up like boring houseguests. These critters have a few things in common; they are unwanted, uninvited, and often bite, leaving itchy reminders of their visit.

The cool and soothing qualities of Lavender come in really handy now. In fact, if you can take only one essential oil on a camping trip with you, it should be Lavender!

Let's deal with avoiding the problem first.

This insect repellent is odorous, in a nice way, to people; in a not-so-nice way to mosquitoes, flies, and fleas. It is, however, made up of oils that are primarily energizing, so it's probably best not to apply it just before bedtime, or you may find your brain working overtime.

Warning: Avoid any contact with eyes, this can sting. And it's best to wash your hands after applying so you don't inadvertently rub your eyes.

INSECT REPELLENT

4 drops Eucalyptus

4 drops Lavender

4 drops Rosemary

4 drops Tea Tree

Mix the above essential oils in any of the following ways:

- Add to 1 teaspoon witch hazel and 4 teaspoons water in a bottle. Shake before applying directly to skin.

- Add to 2 ounces witch hazel and 8 ounces water in a spray bottle. Spray your surroundings and your skin.

- Add to 5 teaspoons olive oil. Rub this oil mixture on your skin, especially on those pulse points on neck, wrists, and ankles which seem to attract such critters.

Warning: Don't use this insect repellent on babies. It's a little too harsh for their tender skin. A few drops of Lavender in olive oil would work nicely for young ones.

You won't be able to get through summer without some bites. Straight Lavender on the bite is a great treatment, but it's also a good idea to keep some of the Bug Bite Mix described below ready-mixed in a bottle for quick and easy application. This recipe also takes advantage of some of the calming properties of Chamomile as well as the anti-itch (antipruritic, according to drugstore labels) properties of Eucalyptus. This, too, can be a somewhat aromatic potion.

BUG BITE MIX

2 drops Chamomile

3 drops Eucalyptus

3 drops Lavender

Blend the oils and use them in any of the following ways:

- Apply straight to the bite.
- Add to a basin of water for washing the affected skin.
- Add the oil blend to 2 tablespoons cider vinegar, which you can dab onto the bites with a cotton ball.

You can also use a drop of Eucalyptus on flea bites.

POISON IVY, POISON OAK, POISON SUMAC

If you have family members susceptible to these three villains, get a good field guide with pictures and learn how to identify them. That will alleviate the problem somewhat, but if someone breaks out in one of those colorful, bumpy, itchy rashes, try the following remedy:

——————————— ❧ ☙ ———————————

POISON WEED RASH RELIEF

5 drops Chamomile

2 drops Geranium

5 drops Lavender

5 drops Tea Tree

Mix the above oils into 1 cup of water. Use in one of the following ways:

❧ Spray this blend on the affected areas. Allow it to dry naturally.

❧ To relieve a large area of skin, you might like a bath. Add 4 drops of the essential oil blend and ¼ cup plain dry oatmeal, to a tepid bath. Soak until you feel better.

❦ Bugs aren't the only cause of summer itching. There's always poison ivy, poison oak, and poison sumac. It must be the gene pool, because my mother and son are both highly allergic to such greenery. Unfortunately for Brian, he doesn't recognize the leaf combinations, and our woodlands often have all three poison plants fairly close together. I know what poison ivy looks like, but I didn't expect the dried-up weeds in the bottom of the garbage can to be poison ivy—and they were in my gloveless hands before I really looked at them. My significant other had been nice enough to weed the area around the garden fence.

—Paula

SUN WORSHIPPING

We all have a friend who thinks she is the sun goddess. Of course, every year, she has to work hard to become the sun goddess once again. Aromatherapy can ease the transition somewhat.

❦ *Not that any of this makes it okay not to use a good sunscreen or sunblock. Judi, as well as anyone else I've ever been to the beach with, knows how I am about sunning. I'm usually that very interesting-looking woman wearing the large straw hat and a burnoose.*

—Paula

Of course you're careful about getting too much sun, but if you still get a little too much, you have to deal with several issues. Your skin is probably hot and itchy, and you might peel. And here the sun goddess cringes; peeling sets her golden aura back several weeks.

You might also want some help for your little ones who get too much sun, in spite of the SPF 100 stuff you probably reapplied several times—before lunch, not to mention all those applications after lunch, and the hat and the T-shirt you made them wear.

The recipe for kids first:

SUNBURN STUFF FOR KIDS

3 drops Chamomile

3 drops Lavender

4 ounces tepid water

Add all ingredients to a spray bottle. Shake and spray.

Sunburn Stuff for Kids will soothe and cool that too-pink skin and make riding home from the beach a lot more comfortable for everyone. If you make this potion ahead of time and store it in your cooler, take it out about an hour before you head home to give it time to warm up so as not to shock that tender, young skin.

Now for the adults (though when it comes to sunning, many of us take on our teenaged persona). Even when you try to be careful, sun happens. You know how it is: You get home from the beach with pink stripes along various body parts. You thought you had sunscreen everywhere, but someone, probably the sunscreen applicator person, missed the striped area. And you certainly know about it later.

You can apply sunburn remedies at any temperature, warm or cold. With children, the difference in skin temperature and cold liquid may be too great and cause them additional, although temporary, discomfort.

The following Sunburn Pain Remedy cools the heat and soothes skin's tendency to itch. The skin-healing qualities of Lavender also help keep the skin moist so it doesn't turn into that papery, peeling stuff.

❦ To be beautiful and to be calm, without mental fear, is the ideal of nature.

—*Richard Jefferies*

———— ❧ ✿ ————

SUNBURN PAIN REMEDY

8 drops Lavender

4 drops Peppermint

8 ounces water

Mix the above ingredients together in a spray bottle. The water can be any temperature that is comfortable for you.

When you know you got burned badly and peeling will probably follow, or you just want to replace some of the moisture that the sun took from your skin, use the following After-Sun Oil.

The following blend cools, soothes, and heals:

———————————— ♋ ♋ ————————————

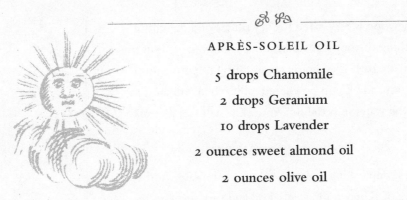

APRÈS-SOLEIL OIL

5 drops Chamomile

2 drops Geranium

10 drops Lavender

2 ounces sweet almond oil

2 ounces olive oil

Mix all the ingredients together in a (preferably plastic) container. Gently rub onto your sunburned parts.

You can also use 1 tablespoon of this mixture as a bath oil.

————————————————————————————————

If you do peel, keep in mind that this is your skin's way of getting rid of a damaged layer and healing. Use Après-Soleil Oil until you stop itching. And remember, itching is often a sign of healing.

SWEET DREAMS

You've worked hard, you've played hard, and now you can't sleep. And you really want to, because tomorrow is probably going to be another day just like today and you need your rest.

Especially for You

Rosewood is very good for dry skin. For a delightful soothing of your skin and mood, soak in the tub in these aromatic bath salts. For extra soothing to your summer dry skin, add ¼ cup powdered milk when you are pouring the water into the tub. Your skin will feel like silk.

FAR, FAR AWAY BATH

Mix ½ cup baking soda and ½ cup Epson salts. Add 10 drops of Rosewood essential oil and mix through the dry ingredients. Store this in a pretty bottle. Use ¼ cup of this mixture to a warm tub of water.

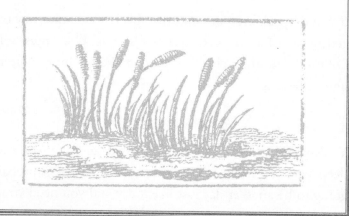

You may remember your grandmother's linen closet smelling of Lavender. And didn't you sleep better at her house than at anybody else's (except home, of course)? Well, maybe Gram thought she was just keeping her linens sweet and fresh-smelling, but the Lavender aroma also helped the lucky person who slipped between those cool, sweet sheets into soothing slumber. (Gram probably also knew that moths don't like the smell of Lavender.)

A little essential oil on a pillowcase or sprayed in bedrooms may be just the ticket to the Land of Nod. These remedies can be used for adults or children because they use the most gentle essential oils: Chamomile, Lavender, and Orange.

Lavender is a very relaxing essential oil, and as you may remember, it is an adaptogen, adapting to your own energy needs. So don't think Lavender in a sleep remedy will keep you awake.

─────────── ✿ ✿ ───────────

SLEEP POTION

3 drops Chamomile

4 drops Lavender

3 drops Orange

5 ounces water

❦ Dreams are the guardians of sleep and not its disturbers.
—*Sigmund Freud*

Mix all ingredients in a spray bottle.

Spray bed clothing and room air before bedtime.

You could put a drop or two of Lavender on the inner hem of your pillowcase, or use a few drops of Lavender in the rinse water for your sheets and pillowcases.

If you want to grow your own Lavender, it's nice to know that intense summer heat and bitter winter cold won't harm the Lavender plant.

Summer is a great time. Your life seems closer to nature, you wear less clothing, things seem just a little freer. Lavender can help you enjoy all these summertime freedoms.

Carry a bottle of Lavender in your pocketbook for quick fixes. Rub a drop between your palms to rid your skin of a fish odor after that great seafood dinner. Put a drop into a public toilet for a nicer experience. Use a few drops and a wet paper towel to wipe down a baby changing table at the airport. Your life will seem cleaner and fresher. Always keep Lavender oil on hand for first aid.

SWEET FEET

The following recipe is about how to relieve hot and bothered feet, not how to create them. If you are in July right now, you certainly know how to create hot and bothered feet yourself. You might even have them right now.

And you know the many ways to get hot and bothered feet: new sneakers, walking barefoot on hot pavement, shopping for too long, or even standing or sitting for too long.

❧ I went to the beach this weekend, and ouch, ouch, ouch, was that sand ever hot! Once again, aromatherapy to the rescue!

—Paula

Time to take a break and treat those poor toes and soles to a soak.

———————— ✿ ✿ ————————

HOT AND BOTHERED FEET REMEDY

1 drop Eucalyptus

3 drops Lavender

1 drop Peppermint

1 teaspoon baking soda

Use in one of the following ways:

- Dissolve the baking soda into a foot basin or pail of tepid water (just above body temperature). Add the Eucalyptus, Lavender, and Peppermint oil to the water. Sit down and soak your feet. This will not only make your feet feel better, but the aroma of the essential oils will make you feel more energetic.

- When you have neither the time nor interest to soak your feet, put the above ingredients into a spray bottle with 1 cup of water. Shake the bottle and spray your feet. Allow them to air dry.

Another problem related to hot and bothered feet is smelly sneakers. You could soak them too, but it's probably more convenient to use Sneaker Freshener.

You will want an empty powder canister, flour shaker, or salt shaker to hold your Sneaker Freshener. This is a good time to go through your bag of recycled containers that we discussed in the first chapter. You can also find some interesting, nonbreakable containers in the kitchenware section of your local department store.

SNEAKER FRESHENER

5 drops Lavender

5 drops Tea Tree

1 tablespoon baking powder or cornstarch

Add the drops of Lavender and Tea Tree to the baking powder (which is more sweetening in nature) or to the cornstarch (which is softer-textured and often used in combination with baby powder). Stir gently to spread the scent of the oils through the powder. Store in a container with a shaker top.

Give the insides of your sneakers a coating of the powder overnight. Empty the sneakers before wearing. Give your sneakers this kind of pampering a few nights in a row and you'll be much better friends in the future!

Why not take care of the entire odiferous foot problem before it spreads to your shoes? The following recipe deodorizes your feet and kills many of the bacteria that help create those smells in the first place.

— ❦ ❦ —

FOOT ODOR REMEDY

4 drops Lavender

2 drops Peppermint

6 drops Rosemary

1 drop Tea Tree

Add the above oils to a warm basin of water. Soak your feet for 10 minutes. Pat dry with a soft towel.

Lavender Forever

Lavender has been called "the angel of healing" and is number one on everyone's list of aromatherapy scents. If you have no other oil in your life, you must have Lavender; and even if you have every oil known to humans, you still must have Lavender.

If you like Lavender, you should plant some. It needs a sunny, dry place in which to grow. Then you can dry out the flowers and fill little bags to hang in your closet or place in your drawers. Make little pillows, or hang the dried herb for

❦ Here's flowers for you,
Hot Lavender, sweet Mints...
—*William Shakespeare*

a cozy country feeling. Or stuff teddy bears to sleep with . . . well, you get the picture.

There are lots of ways to include Lavender in your life. You'll think of some more.

In thinking of additional indulgent uses of Lavender, I realized that just about every blend I have ever made was enhanced when I added Lavender to it. So experiment freely with Lavender; it might just be that extra-special addition you were looking for.

—Judi

OIL OF THE MONTH

Peppermint

Mentha x piperita

Ah, summer, what power you have to make us
suffer and like it.

—*Russell Baker*

school clothes already!

vacation by the sea

steamy romance novels

walk along the beach, seashell-finding

record–breaking heatwave

running through the sprinkler

conversations in the cool of the night

The Lazy, Hazy Days of Summer

Whoever wrote those words certainly did not live in our decade. People today cannot afford the luxury of lazy summer days—crazy is more like it. We continually face the challenge of adjusting our work schedules to accommodate summer camp, visits to the pool or ocean, and late curfews (or lack thereof). We also have to be more creative in meal planning—the torrid temperatures of August call for light, easy, eat-on-the-run meals. And we never feel anything less than wilted, peeling our sweat-soaked clothes off at day's end. And how can we forget the forever-full laundry basket that contains half the sand from the local beach? This is a vacation?

In August it seems that we are always running here or there. Playing tennis in the early morning before the humidity takes over. Then running into the air-conditioned freeze of the office. Hurrying after work for a few hours of beach fun with the kids. We're exhausted just thinking about it!

This hectic lifestyle often results in not taking proper care of ourselves. We may not eat well or take time for stress-reducing relaxation. For these reasons especially, we need to make sure we include aromatherapy in our lives.

So crazy—yes. Lazy—not for a minute. That is why this month we are featuring the flexible, uplifting properties of Peppermint—perfect for the dog-days of summer.

Peppermint

This versatile essence comes from the peppermint plant. You can actually feel the coolness of mint by putting your hand near a mint plant on a hot sunny day. Ancient cultures used Peppermint for centuries, no doubt because of its extremely useful health-promoting properties.

Peppermint is best known for its qualities to treat digestive issues such as flatulence, nausea, indigestion, liver problems, vomiting, cramps, and motion sickness. But it is also very effective in treating fevers, flu, headaches, and migraines.

Peppermint's wonderful anti-inflammatory properties are great in helping to reduce swelling and strengthen the skin's natural defenses. You can treat the symptoms of muscle and joint pain resulting from overexertion tenderly and effectively with this oil.

On an emotional level, Peppermint sharpens the conscious mind, increasing concentration and memory, thus allowing you to become clearheaded and to feel your spirits revive.

The disinfectant and antiseptic properties of Peppermint make it a must in every first-aid kit because it relieves insect bites, repels fleas and ants, and alleviates bad breath at its main sources (stomach and mouth). It also helps ease toothaches.

🌿 To live happily is an inward power of the soul.

—*Marcus Aurelius*

Peppermint is used in many products you are already aware of. Often mouthwash, cold and cough syrups, and muscle pain rubs contain Peppermint, either as the natural essence or in a synthetic form.

Doesn't Peppermint sound like the perfect oil to feature this month? It can help us feel less hazy, invigorate us when we're lazy, and even stabilize us when we're crazy responding to the many vigors of August.

Warning: Peppermint is not recommended to use with homeopathic treatment. Peppermint may also irritate the mucous membranes of individuals with hay fever.

Remedies

Peppermint is a powerful oil that is effective in small doses. Just add a drop or two to a glass of water for a mouthwash, into some of your favorite recipes, or in a massage blend for sore muscles. You'll find that Peppermint is versatile and refreshing.

If scheduling conflicts leave you feeling hectic, out of control, or overwrought, you could certainly use a safe, energizing way to get rid of pounding headaches. Try this recipe.

━━━━━━━━━━━ ❧ ℘ℓ℘ ━━━━━━━━━━━

HEADACHE REMEDY

1 drop Peppermint

Massage one drop into your temples. Put your feet up for a few minutes, and envision yourself in a quiet, calm, refreshing place. Let the essence of Peppermint take you and the pain away from it all.

Warning: Avoid the eye area. Peppermint will sting if it gets in your eyes.

SOMETHING CALMER

If Peppermint is too invigorating for your tension headaches, a single drop of Lavender is a gentler solution. Of course, don't forget the rest and relaxation part of the recipe.

SUMMER SPORTS

There is so much activity in the summer: tennis, jogging, and running on the beach. With the intense heat, it is important to stay hydrated and not overdo it. For people who do overdo it, we designed the blend below.

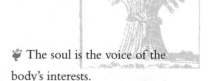

❧ The soul is the voice of the body's interests.

—*George Santayana*

❧ I love running early on an August day while there is still just a touch of morning freshness, but I usually wilt in the steamy afternoons. Now, with a little help from Peppermint, I get some summertime relief in the form of uplifting blends.

—Judi

MUSCLE RUB

4 drops Lavender

3 drops Peppermint

5 drops Rosemary

Mix oils into 2 tablespoons of vegetable oil. Starting with the feet, massage feet and legs.

For the athlete who goes a little too close to that edge, whether it be from jogging, tennis, or water sports, the next two recipes are real treats: the first deals with inflamed joints and the second is great for sprains.

INFLAMMATION SOOTHER

10 drops Chamomile

5 drops Eucalyptus

3 drops Lavender

7 drops Peppermint

5 drops Rosemary

Mix oils into 2 tablespoons of vegetable oil. Massage into inflamed area.

---- ❧ ❧ ----

MUSCLE SPRAIN REMEDY

10 drops Eucalyptus

10 drops Peppermint

10 drops Rosemary

Mix oils into 2 tablespoons of vegetable oil. Cool sprain with ice pack for 20 minutes, then massage with blend.

UGH, I'M HOT

Lavender, Chamomile, Peppermint, and Geranium are great for heat exhaustion.

THE WILTED WARRIOR

You can use this all-purpose spray, which includes Peppermint, throughout your entire house. Spritz the room to lighten the mugginess. Add a few drops to the laundry to freshen your clothes. In both cases, you'll feel your droopy feelings brighten.

---- ❧ ❧ ----

ALL-PURPOSE SPRAY

4 drops Lavender

2 drops Peppermint

2 drops Tea Tree

Mix oils into 2 cups of water.

❦ Now we're talking. My idea of a physically fit summer is not to sweat. Give me those cooling blends. You won't find me running around in the hot sun.

—Paula

❦ I use the following recipe in two very different ways: first as an insect repellent and also as a room spray to remove the stifling air the air conditioner can't remove.

—Judi

❦ Spray liberally in the areas in which "the ants are marching one by one" and then you can say "hurrah" when you see them no longer.

—Judi

Especially for You

Indian Summer
Nights when gauze curtains flutter
From the nighttime breeze

August can be such a never-ending, lazy, hot month. You need a secret pleasure, possibly one to share with your love. Sandalwood, with its Oriental whispers, is just the pleasure you need.

Sandalwood evokes the very place it's from—India. Its name comes from the Sanskrit word *chandana*. It smells exotic and mysterious. It's often used in meditation because it clears your thinking and helps center you. Sandalwood is also very grounding to your emotions, as many woods are. That makes it perfect for the following massage oil, a blend that has a warm lingering fragrance you will remember and love.

INDIAN EVENING MASSAGE

2 drops Sandalwood and 3 drops Orange (or Bergamot if you have it). Mix the essential oils into 2 tablespoons canola oil to use as a massage oil. Take some unhurried time with your love. Candles and easy far-away music set a beautiful scene for you.

Just like Lemon, Lavender, and Geranium, Peppermint is an adaptogen, adapting to your needs.

TASTY TREATMENTS

Peppermint is one oil that is frequently used in beverages and cooking. You are probably also familiar with the taste of Peppermint in your favorite mouthwash.

There are many terrific mouthwash combinations you can make using other oils from your basic kit. As you become more familiar with the properties of the oils, experiment to find the mouthwash that best suits your preferences. You might also include Fennel or Orange. This recipe is one that has gotten "tasteful" reviews.

───────── ⚘ ⚘ ─────────

MOUTHWASH

4 drops Lemon

2 drops Peppermint

Mix oils into 2 cups of distilled water (or water you have boiled and allowed to cool). Don't knock it until you've tried it. The flavoring differences between Peppermint and Lemon make a refreshing, effective, and tasty brew.

One morning I was getting ready for a very important business meeting and discovered I was out of my favorite mouthwash. Instead of running around in a panic trying to find a pharmacy open at 5:00 A.M., I calmly blended the following recipe.
—Judi

And she also saved money and created an alcohol-free mouthwash.
—Paula

TOOTHACHE AID

For a toothache, put 1 drop of Peppermint and 1 drop of Chamomile into 2 ounces of water. Soak a cotton ball in the solution and apply to tooth and gum.

Warning: Should you decide to prepare a mouthwash for your children (check with your dentist first), it is recommended that you do not use Peppermint. The strength of the oil may not be tolerated well by small children.

To lighten up a summer beverage, add a drop of Peppermint and imagine yourself sipping mint juleps while sitting out on the verandah overlooking the back forty. (Oh, all right, this may be a bit much, but that's what fantasies are for.) You may also want to add a drop to a marinade for seafood you are preparing on the barbecue.

Warning: Do not exceed recommended drops when taking Peppermint orally; overdose may cause stomach or intestinal irritation.

THE VACATION BLUES

Your vacation has finally arrived! You are at your dream cottage at the beach ready for a week of sun, fun, and relaxation. However, there are days when the weather suggests you stay inside and overindulge with card games, videos, and a full range of junk food (the fifth food group). As you can imagine, several members of your vacationing group may be struck with sour stomachs.

_____ ✄ ✄ _____

TUMMY TROUBLES BE GONE

1 drop Eucalyptus

1 drop Peppermint

2 drops Rosemary

Mix oils into 2 tablespoons of a base oil and massage the stomach. Remember, you want to relax and slow yourself down to get the best benefit from this blend. You should also drink a lot of water so you don't get dehydrated.

STOMACHACHE HELPER

For a stomachache, put 15 drops of Peppermint into 2 tablespoons of vegetable oil and massage in a clockwise direction around the belly button and back.

On the days when the sun does cooperate, you may overindulge in the sun. If so, use the following recipe.

❧ That is especially a problem when you have nine people and only one bathroom, as we did last summer. Let this next recipe help you make it through.

—Paula

❧ You can also make a blend that you can take orally. An alternative to our "Tummy Troubles Be Gone" blend: put 1 drop of Peppermint into a teaspoon of honey and dilute in a glass of warm water; sip slowly.

—Judi

＆ ℰ

BEACH REVIVER

4 drops Lavender

1 drop Peppermint

2 drops Rosemary

Mix the oils with a pint of water to use as a spritzer at the beach or pool to revive yourself. The fragrance will lighten and refresh you.

RELIEF FOR TOO MUCH SUN

Lavender, Eucalyptus, Peppermint, and Chamomile are all great oils for sunburns and the effects of too much sun.

HELPFUL HINTS

To store some of your favorite oils when you travel, we found a great little makeup bag. It has a plastic inside lining and is large enough to fit travel-size glass containers of each of our most frequently used oils. You might want to get one for yourself.

When labeling your blends, be sure to adhere the label to the bottle, not the cap. Caps can accidentally be placed on the wrong bottle.

❧ I put labels on the bottom of the bottle. This way, if some of the oil spills over the sides, I can wipe it clean without removing the label.
—Judi

More Mint

Mint spreads like wildfire. Plant a little bit and it sends out root sprouts and takes over its space, often crowding out nearby plants. (Not very nice for the other nearby members of your herb garden, but mint plants are also useful.) Plant some around your foundation to keep ants away. And they're attractive and inexpensive.

Mint comes in many varieties: Peppermint, Spearmint, Pineapple Mint, Applemint, Bergamot Mint, and Ginger Mint are a few you can find at your local nursery. Each smells and looks a little different.

You can use mint to make tea or use it as flavoring for frosting, jellies, and candies. When cooking, keep Peppermint in mind for seasoning, especially with lamb.

A potpourri ball containing mint is great in your stored clothes closet. Dry leaves from your mint plants and add them to commercially available potpourri. Hang this in a little net bag from a hanger.

If you like Peppermint, you'll probably also like Spearmint or Birch, which smells like Wintergreen (real Wintergreen oil is toxic—poisonous—so we strongly recommend that you do not buy it).

As we can all appreciate, knowledge is power. Enjoy your knowledge, enjoy these recipes, enjoy Peppermint, enjoy August, and most of all, enjoy your health.

Join the whole creation of animate things in a deep, heart-felt joy that you are alive, that you see the sun, that you are in this glorious earth which nature has made so beautiful, and which is yours to enjoy.

—*Sir William Osler*

Especially for You

You will find that Sandalwood mixes well with many of the basic twelve oils as well as with the luxury oils. Try it in place of Cedar for a more evocative effect in some of the pampering and relaxing blends.

ARABIAN BREEZES

2 drops Sandalwood, 2 drops Cedar, 2 drops Lavender, 2 drops Ylang-Ylang. Mix these essential oils together and use just one drop on your pulse points. Sandalwood has great staying power and this scent will last a long time.

a Vine

OIL OF THE MONTH

Rosemary

Rosmarinus officinalis

Rosemary is for remembrance
Between us day and night,
Wishing that I may always have
You present in my sight.

—*Old Ballad*

back to school!

another year begins

new and overflowing schedules

buses to catch, buses to greet

plaid flannel shirts—on sale!

cheerleaders practicing

homework, homework, homework

brisk evenings and chilly mornings

great sleeping weather!

Hooray!
Fall Is Here

It's finally September. How you must marvel that you ever felt summer would go on forever. That dreaminess is now gone, replaced by a faster pace and lists of things to do. And if your contemplative summer hasn't already left, the first cool mornings after your vacation certainly will escort it away.

With the departure of any leisure time you managed to have during the summer, you may now feel a new sense of purpose: new things to do, new projects, new goals—new needs for energy. Maybe it's that first day of school for your (sob) kindergartner, or shopping with your college-bound teenagers for their dorm decorating needs. This is all new to you, too.

You will find, with all your new fall activities, many areas in which aromatherapy can be a welcome and pleasant helper. All the things you have to do and all the things you have to think about may not match your energy level. New activities use new muscles that may not have been exercised in months. A new season and a new schedule (more like several schedules, really—every member of your household will have their own schedule, no doubt) bring new hygiene concerns.

The oil for September, with all its changes, is Rosemary. This oil will help you rev up your system to meet all the challenges September can bring your way.

🌿 For Spring and Autumn, sun and rain, the blessedness of work-filled days, for blooming rose and garnered grain, Take, Lord, my praise.

—*George Burt Lake*

Rosemary

Rosemary is one of the oldest essential oils; it was used in ancient Egypt, Greece, and Rome for mental stimulation, cleansing, and purification. This oil, which is a natural antiseptic, disinfectant, and detoxifier, also stimulates the immune system.

Rosemary, with its clean and strong fragrance, is steam-distilled from the flowers and needle-like leaves of the herb. The "fingerprint" of Rosemary, the leaves and flowers it comes from, tell us it can affect respiration and the brain or emotions. In fact, Rosemary is stimulating to both mind and body.

The stimulating properties of Rosemary make it a natural aid in combating mental fatigue and enhancing concentration as it helps you fight procrastination and forgetfulness. It stimulates the brain in the area that assists in logical thinking, math, and numbers—something that is particularly useful in September.

In Victorian times, women used to rinse their dark hair in Rosemary rinse to enhance its color and shine.

Rosemary blends well with Cedar, Clary Sage, Lemon, Eucalyptus, Peppermint, and Pine.

Warning: Keep Rosemary (or any essential oil) away from your eyes. If you do accidentally get some in your eyes, rinse your eyes with water until the stinging goes away. Do not use Rose-

mary oil if you are pregnant or epileptic. We do not recommend
Rosemary oil for use on infants, as it is rather strong for them.

Remedies

In this chapter, you can find Rosemary-based remedies that take advantage of its stimulating properties for waking up and enhancing concentration and memory.

Rosemary's circulatory properties can be used to alleviate the sore muscles and sports pain you will run into now that fall is here. Speaking of sports, Rosemary can also help with that locker-room smell that will be coming home from the gym.

And because of its usefulness in beauty products, you can incorporate Rosemary into your own routine, in dandruff shampoo, as a hair conditioner, and even as a toner for oily skin.

GOOOOD MORNING, SEPTEMBER!

Oh, that first Monday morning after vacation! For many of us it seems like this is truly the beginning of fall. The following hint can help you hit the ground running:

EYE OPENER

A few drops of Rosemary in a morning shower can give you a fresh start to your day.

And since, by the end of that first Monday after vacation,

🌱 Great mother of big apples
it is a pretty world.
　　　　—*Kenneth Patchen*

you'll feel as though you did hit the ground running, try the following hint for an energizing end to your day:

ENERGIZING DAY'S END

A few drops of Rosemary in a bath after a physically challenging day really revs up those muscles.

The circulating and stimulating properties of Rosemary make it a perfect aid for those of you who are not morning people, and we do know what we're talking about. Rosemary helps your blood get going as well as your brain.

✣ Truth is, all my Mondays seem to feel that way. And was it "hit the ground running" or "hit the wall running"? Because by the end of some days, I feel like I hit a wall.
—Paula

—————— ⅋ ——————

GROUCH PREVENTION

2 drops Lavender

2 drops Lemon

2 drops Peppermint

6 drops Rosemary

6 drops Tea Tree

✣ If you, like me, have a little trouble getting started in the morning, try the following blend to wake up.
—Paula

Mix all oils together. Use the blend in one of these ways:

↬ Mix into 16 ounces of water and spray the air around the potential grouch as soon as he or she (or you) get up.

↬ Mix the essential oils into 2 tablespoons of any vegetable oil to use as a body oil after showering.

Caught without any Grouch Prevention? Try the hint below in this kind of emergency:

QUICK SHOWER PICK-ME-UP

Shower in cool water. Just before you finish, add a drop or two of Rosemary to your face cloth and rub it all over— but not on your eyes. This will tingle and the scent will sharpen your wits for the day to come.

THOUGHT-PROVOKING ROSEMARY

Rosemary has been known to stimulate memory for so long that ancient Greek and Roman students wore Rosemary wreaths when they studied. Rather than wearing headgear when you study, try this recipe in an air spray:

———————————————— ঙ ৯৯ ————————————————

CONCENTRATION BLEND

2 drops Cedar

1 drop Eucalyptus

4 drops Lavender

2 drops Orange

2 drops Rosemary

Mix all oils together.

Add the essential oils to 16 ounces of water and use as a room spray before you sit down to study. Refresh the room from time to time as you study.

DRIVING ALERT

Before driving in the night, put two drops of Rosemary on a tissue and place it in your pocket or attach it to your visor to help you stay alert the whole ride home.

AND ONE AND TWO

Rosemary's high hydrogen content makes it warming and stimulating—it really gets your blood moving. This is exactly why it is so good to help deal with muscle aches and pains. This circulatory effect of Rosemary makes it particularly useful in a massage for sore muscles you may have overwhelmed with your fall activities.

Rosemary is one of the essential oils I always carry with me. In the afternoon when lunch begins to lull me to sleep or when I'm driving at night, I take a deep breath or two of the oil.

—Paula

MUSCLE RUB

2 drops Lavender

2 drops Lemon

2 drops Peppermint

4 drops Rosemary

2 teaspoons canola oil

Mix essential oils with vegetable oil. Slowly massage this blend into aching muscles.

Especially for You

Happy Birthday child
New things and school now begin
Stay calm and open

Patchouli has a musky, earthy aroma that eases worries and brings a sense of calm. So when getting the kids back to school becomes hectic and chaotic, let Patchouli work for you. Patchouli comes from the leaves of the Pogostemon patchouli plant, a member of the mint family. At one time Patchouli was used to protect clothing from moths, so it can have an old-fashioned feeling to it. Patchouli comes from India where it was used to scent (and protect) Paisley shawls. It is also an ingredient of India ink.

This room spray is one that Judi's daughter (whose birthday is in September) loves . We hope you enjoy it too.

SLEEP SUPPORTER

To a pint of water, add 2 drops of Patchouli, 2 drops of Orange, 2 drops of Clary Sage, and 2 drops of Lavender.

GOING FOR THE BURN

Occasionally, and you may find this hard to believe, you can really overdo it with sports or exercise.

This time you need something that will work on revving up the circulation of the offending area (like the recipe for Muscle Rub) along with something soothing, like Chamomile.

Truth is, sometimes you can pull something vital, just by trying to grasp something that's a little bit too far out of your range. Like that glass way in the back of the cabinet.

—Paula

SPORTS PAIN REMEDY

5 drops Chamomile

5 drops Lavender

5 drops Lemon

5 drops Peppermint

10 drops Rosemary

Mix all essential oils together.

Add them to 2 tablespoons olive oil. Gently massage this into painful muscles.

The Sports Pain Remedy uses a higher concentration of essential oils to base oil because you are dealing with a higher concentration of sensation—it hurts! Be very gentle as you massage the painful area, but be generous with the blend.

HAIR! HAIR!

Rosemary is a true friend to hair. It stimulates and conditions the skin of the scalp and stimulates blood flow to the scalp, which in turn strengthens the roots and shafts of hair.

The following hair moisturizer is actually an oil treatment for your hair. It will restore shine and cut down on static electricity, which may be a problem for those of you with dry hair. Hair Moisturizer works very well on hair that has been chemically treated with perms or colorings. Even your hairdresser will be impressed.

A common additive to herbal shampoos, Rosemary helps your hair grow healthier and stronger. It makes dark hair shine, which is what women from Victorian times used it for.

✿ I'm usually static-prone anyway. And in the fall and winter, my long hair used to drive me crazy! When it's cold outside and dry inside, I pamper my hair with the following treatment once every one or two weeks.

—Paula

HAIR MOISTURIZER

8 drops Cedar

8 drops Lavender

12 drops Rosemary

Mix all oils together. Add the essential oils to 2 tablespoons olive oil. This makes enough of the blend for several applications.

Pour about a teaspoon of the blend into the palm of your hand. Warm it by rubbing your palms together. Massage your head, hair, and scalp with the blend. Put a shower cap or warm towel on your head and leave it for fifteen minutes to let the warmth increase your hair's absorption of the blend.

Wash your hair as you normally would. You may want to shampoo and rinse twice.

The hair rinse below makes your hair look healthier and smell great, too.

———— ✄ ✁ ————

RINSE FOR DARK HAIR

15 drops Cedar

15 drops Rosemary

Mix oils together and add to 8 ounces of liquid hair conditioner.

Apply as you would any conditioner after you have rinsed the shampoo from your hair.

You might be less than happy with your hair because you have the telltale flakes of dandruff. Use the Flake-Free Shampoo in the following recipe to rev up your scalp and help free it from white flakes.

🐚 A change in the weather is enough to renew the world and ourselves.

—*Marcel Proust*

Especially for You

Because Patchouli eases worries and brings calm, it's great in a room spray to keep in the office and use when needed.

CALMING SPRAY

Put 2 drops of Patchouli, 2 drops of Clary Sage, and 2 drops of Lavender into a pint of water and place in a spray bottle.

&ℰ ℱ&

FLAKE-FREE SHAMPOO

20 drops Eucalyptus

20 drops Lemon

30 drops Rosemary

8 ounces baby shampoo

Mix the oils together and add to the baby shampoo. This
shampoo will smell and feel strong as you apply it to your
hair. Once you have lathered up, leave it in your hair for
five minutes so the essential oils can be absorbed into your
scalp. Feel that tingle? It's starting to work.

CHANGES OF THE SKIN

As the weather changes, your skin's needs also change. Skin
you thought was too oily just a few weeks ago now seems
dry. Use the toner below before you apply your moisturizer.

&ℰ ℱ&

DRY SKIN TONER

3 drops Clary Sage

2 drops Geranium

1 drop Lavender

2 drops Rosemary

Mix the oils together.

🌿 Awake O north wind, and
come thou south! Blow upon my
garden that the spices thereof
may flow out . . . .

—Song of Solomon 4:16

Add to 4 tablespoons springwater. Splash skin before applying moisturizer.

Put the above toner into a spray bottle and store the bottle in the refrigerator. This makes a refreshing spritz for your face after exercise.

CHANGES OF THE SEASONS

Fall allergies are often as inhibiting as spring allergies. You might experience the same difficulty in breathing and that dry, hacking cough might keep you up all night. The following blend in a vaporizer might be just what you need to help clear the air.

ALLERGY RELIEF

3 drops Eucalyptus

2 drops Lavender

1 drop Peppermint

2 drops Rosemary

Mix the oils together.

Add to a full cool-mist vaporizer.

More Rosemary Power

The clean, crisp smell of Rosemary is certainly representative of this clean, crisp month. Take Rosemary with you to meet the pace of September. It provides a quick, natural hit of energy, more healthy than a speedy cup of coffee! Because of the brain-energizing qualities of Rosemary, you won't want to make use of it directly before bedtime or you'll find your mind much too busy to fall asleep.

If you like Rosemary, you might also like Thyme, which has a similar sharp scent and also comes from the leaves of the herb. Grow the herbs in your garden or on your windowsill.

Cook with these herbs, too. Try the "Simon and Garfunkel" herbal mix: Parsley, Sage, Rosemary, and Thyme. It's great in chicken pie—a perfect autumn supper.

🌷 Flowers leave some of their fragrance in the hand that bestows them.

—*Chinese proverb*

OIL OF THE MONTH

Tea Tree

Melaleuca alternifolia

Nature gives to every time and season some

beauties of its own....

—*Charles Dickens*

beautiful leaves

trick or treat!

just a sweater, it's warm today

pumpkin patches, carving, and salted seeds

rustling leaves in the gutter all the way home

check out the scenery

great costumes

Trick or Treat

October is such a sparkling month, full of many treats. The cool, crisp morning air makes your lungs tingle with each deep breath. The explosion of colors is autumn's trademark and October's signature. The rustle of leaves as you walk through the park tickles your ears, and nature's scent as it prepares for the long hibernation of winter tantalizes you, making you remember the autumns of long ago.

The laughter of schoolchildren playing outside, enjoying every moment of this brisk month, makes you feel like jumping into a pile of leaves. And of course, we all share in the anticipation and enjoyment of Halloween.

Along with these many treats, October also brings us some unique tricks that aromatherapy can help with. Now that the windows are closed in the evening, germs and viruses start nesting, particularly in classrooms but also in your home. Every sniffle and cold that one child gets is shared with the rest of the family. Keep a watchful eye out for sniffles, sore throats, and those dreaded earaches. Many of us suffer from change-in-the-season congestion; we find our energy level zapped out before the day is gone.

In addition, our bodies start to go through their seasonal change as our skin tries to adjust from the past months' humidity to the dry, cool air of autumn. It seems that everyone in the family, including pets, is particularly sensitive to seasonal changes.

🐾 Speak out, whisper not,
Here bloweth thyme and
    bergamot,
Softly on thee every hour
Secret herbs their spices shower,
Dark-spiked rosemary and
    myrrh,
Lean-stalked, purple lavender....
        —*Walter de la Mare*

Fortunately, with Tea Tree, the oil for October, you can trick some of these predicaments and treat yourself to a refreshing and enjoyable month.

Tea Tree

Tea Tree enjoys a long and memorable history. The tree, indigenous to Australia, has been used in medications for centuries. Today Tea Tree is the subject of a great deal of international research.

Known as the "miracle oil," it is regarded as the single most effective and nontoxic antibacterial and antifungal essential oil. It is similar to Lavender in that it also has universal healing properties.

In the eighteenth century in Australia, Captain Cook and his mates wanted to drink a refreshing herb tea. They chose the fragrant leaves of the Tea Tree that grew in swampy regions.

During World War II, Tea Tree oil was considered such a necessity that those people who cut and produced Tea Tree were exempt from war service until sufficient reserves had been accumulated to be included in first aid kits for the Army and Navy.

Tea Tree also has a fanciful life-cycle. The oil, which has a yellowish color, is derived from narrow-leafed, paper bark trees that grow twenty feet high and thrive in flood-prone wetlands. Because no vehicles can enter the swampy regions

where Tea Tree grows, harvesting the leaves is very laborious. Cutters use lightweight, razor-sharp machetes to cut and strip the leaves from the branches; once cut, the leaves grow back in six months!

Tea Tree is strongest as a fungicide, antiseptic, and as a respiratory aid. Tea Tree, which is in the same botanical family as Eucalyptus, has a spicy, strong, and fresh fragrance.

The same sharp scents that the month of October offers us make Tea Tree the perfect oil for this month.

Remedies

Versatile Tea Tree offers many healing attributes. In this chapter, we explore the antiviral comforts of the oil in blends for respiratory concerns such as coughs, colds, and sniffles. After you've blended Tea Tree with a base oil, massage the affected area and enjoy immediate and long-term relief. Tea Tree is also effective in a diffuser, vaporizer, or simply in a pot of boiling water to clear the air, open nasal passages, and attack germs.

We also look at its antifungal assistance in treating athlete's foot, foot odor, and jock itch. Again, you can use Tea Tree in either a base oil or water to treat these symptoms.

Its antiseptic properties make it great for warding off cold sores, swollen glands, bites, cuts, toothaches, and other infections.

I finally figured out the only reason to be alive is to enjoy it.
—*Rita Mae Brown*

Tea Tree works well to ward off skin and scalp problems such as rashes and dandruff. And finally, Tea Tree is great to use as a flea repellent and an anti-itch shampoo for the four-legged members of your family. You can find pet shampoo with Tea Tree essential oil already added to it at the pet store, but you'll save a lot by making your pet his own at home.

KEEP IT CLOSE AT HAND

Keep a supply of Tea Tree on hand at all times. Store the pure oil in glass containers in a cool, dark place. The oil can dissolve certain plastics.

MOMMY, MY NOSE IS DRIPPING

Tea Tree blends well with Eucalyptus, Peppermint, Rosemary, and Lavender to treat respiratory conditions. Use the following recipe in a diffuser or vaporizer during the day and night.

You can also turn a blend into an inhaler by placing a few drops on a cotton ball and tucking it into the pillowcase. This would certainly make sweet dreams. And when you're frustrated by the exhaustion of a fever, a few drops of a blend in a bath provide a feeling of calm to offset fatigue.

This formula is effective in dealing with minor colds. For children—or adults, for that matter—who have more

When my daughter comes to me with a runny nose, congestion in her chest, and a fever, I immediately reach for my Tea Tree.

—Judi

deep-seated respiratory problems, such as bronchitis, the Cough-Ender blend that follows this recipe might be more of what you need.

―――――――――――――― ❧ ❧ ――――――――――――――

RESPIRATORY AILMENTS REMEDY

10 drops Eucalyptus

10 drops Lavender

10 drops Rosemary

10 drops Tea Tree

Mix all oils together. Use your blend in any of the following ways:

- ❧ Use 3 drops in a diffuser during the day. After one use, refresh the water and add 3 drops of the blend for use at night.

- ❧ Put 2 drops on a cotton ball and tuck inside the child's pillow.

- ❧ Use 1 drop in a tub of warm water for a pleasant bath.

CARE AWAY FROM HOME

When your children are at school or daycare, use 1 drop of the blend on a tissue. Tuck it their shirt pocket to give them protection from germs and viruses all day long.

COUGH-ENDER

10 drops Chamomile

10 drops Eucalyptus

10 drops Lavender

10 drops Rosemary

10 drops Tea Tree

Mix all oils together. Use this blend in either of these ways:

- Use 3 drops in a diffuser during the day. After one use, refresh the water and add 3 drops of the blend for use at night.
- Mix between 10 and 20 drops of the blend in 2 tablespoons vegetable oil to massage your child's chest and back (lung area) three times a day.

This blend has a strong fragrance. Start the massage with ten drops of the blend in the base oil, then evaluate the scent. If it is pleasing to you, you're all set. If it seems a bit mild, increase the drops of the blend, but do not exceed twenty drops.

Of course, we know that those deep coughs that rattle your chest and set off alarm bells occur only in the middle of the night. So you might want to make these blends up before the cold season really strikes. This way when you

There is no need to go to India or anywhere else to find peace. You will find that deep place of silence right in your room, your garden, or even your bathtub.

—*Elisabeth Kübler-Ross*

Especially for You

Comfort caresses
Childhood's call reaches back now
Carefree! Sweet and warm

Vanilla, the symbol of comfort food, is derived from the bean of a tropical orchid. This sweet, soothing aroma is equally appealing to men and women. It is said that deer will leave the protection of the forest to approach the fragrance of Vanilla.

Vanilla mixes well with Lavender, Orange, Lemon, and Cedar. You can also use Vanilla essential oil in cooking, but it's a lot more powerful than Vanilla extract so use sparingly. Vanilla is calming and relaxing. Try out this air spray for your home. Can't you just feel that crisp autumn air outside and your safe, cozy home inside? Spray the air, pillows, blankets, and curtains. Snuggle in for fall.

ORIGINAL COMFORT SPRAY

Mix 8 drops Lavender, 3 drops Vanilla, 3 drops Ylang-Ylang, 10 drops Orange, and 8 drops Cedar essential oils. Add ¼ cup warm water (to disperse the vanilla oil which seems to stay together in cold water and not mix with the other oils or the water). Add 1¾ cups water and use as an air spray—delicious and comforting.

are stumbling around at 3:00 A.M., you'll have immediate access to a soothing and effective remedy for bronchial difficulties.

A constant complaint in the locker room at my gym is the problem of athlete's foot—and the itch and odor associated with it. Itch and odor also strike the men's locker room, but it's not the feet that are affected.

—Judi

STOP THE ITCH, I WANT TO GET OFF

Tea Tree is a must for any first aid kit, and for every gym bag. Its antifungal attributes make it a super oil for these specific concerns.

ANTI-ITCH REMEDY

10 drops Lavender

10 drops Tea Tree

Mix oils together.

Put 5 drops of the blend in a quart of water. Add 1 cup of salt and soak your feet for a good twenty minutes.

You might find that this soothing bath soak is enough to take care of your itching. Try it for three days in a row. If you find that you need more help in combating this ailment, go on to the next recipe.

FOOT FIXER

6 drops Lavender

3 drops Lemon

12 drops Tea Tree

Mix oils together.

The recommended base oil for this massage is borage seed, evening primrose, and vitamin E (available in most health food stores).

Add the oils to 2 tablespoons of the combination base oil, and massage your feet daily after the foot soak.

To complement the above two solutions to fungal problems of the feet, treat your tootsies to a refreshing foot spritz.

FOOT SPRITZ

10 drops Lavender

10 drops Peppermint

10 drops Rosemary

10 drops Tea Tree

Mix oils together.

🌱 Each day is born anew for those who take it rightly.
—*James Russell Lowell*

Put 8 drops of the blend into a quart of water. Use a spray bottle to give your feet a refreshing lift and deter the odors often associated with foot problems.

SENSITIVE ITCHES

To combat jock itch, use 2 drops of Tea Tree in a bowl of water and wash the affected area. Then use 2 drops of Tea Tree mixed into 1 teaspoon of vegetable oil and apply to area. Repeat this every morning and evening for five days.

OUCH, OUCH, OUCH

Tea Tree is very low in toxicity in spite of its strength in odor. Therefore, it can be applied directly to the skin undiluted, and is very useful for assisting and speeding all healing, especially those little cuts and scrapes, and even toothaches.

It is here that Lavender, known as the "angel of healing" and Tea Tree, know as the "miracle oil" work so well together.

One of my favorite October activities is hiking. There is so much to learn as you explore the wonders of nature, and the exhilarating exercise on a cool day is great for your mental health. However, when I am trudging around the mountains and forests, I almost always return with scrapes from loose branches or even a callous from too much of a good thing.

—Judi

CUTS AND SCRAPES REMEDY

Lavender

Tea Tree

1. Put 2 drops of Tea Tree and 5 drops of Lavender into 2 cups warm water to bathe the wound.

My toddler got all four molars at once. On the one hand, it was a blessing because it was done and over with. On the other hand, I could have used more than two hours sleep at night. Once again, aromatherapy came to the rescue.

—Judi

2. Then apply 1 drop Tea Tree and 2 drops Lavender directly to the boo-boo.

SERIOUS HEALING HELP

For more severe cuts that require additional attention, put 4 drops of Tea Tree and 5 drops of Lavender directly on the cut. The low toxicity of Tea Tree and Lavender allows them to be used undiluted.

TOOTHACHE REMEDY

2 drops Chamomile

7 drops Tea Tree

Mix oils together; put 1 drop of the blend on your fingertip and rub on the gum.

HEALING IS ALWAYS SKIN DEEP

Tea Tree is used commercially in soaps, shampoo, antiseptic cream, douche, toothpaste, deodorant, and anti-itch pet shampoo. The oil penetrates to help oxygenate skin cells while aiding in the repair of damaged skin. Tea Tree is approved by the U.S. government for use in cosmetic formulations.

Here is a terrific recipe that applies to a variety of skin care issues for young and old alike.

SKIN CLEANSER AND SOOTHER

4 drops Chamomile

6 drops Geranium

6 drops Lavender

4 drops Lemon

2 drops Tea Tree

Mix oils together. Use the blend in one of the following ways:

- Put 4 drops of the blend into 1 cup of water. Use a spray bottle to apply the spray to your face for toning and refreshing. Leave on for a few minutes, and then gently wipe face with cotton balls.

- For dry skin, put 12 drops of the blend into 2 table-spoons of vegetable oil and massage affected area. This has proven to be quite effective for chapped hands.

PRIVATE PROTECTION

After shaving or waxing, either use the spray or apply several undiluted drops of the blend to newly shaved or waxed area to cut down on redness and swelling.

I've found that a light mist of this blend as a spray is very effective in treating diaper rash and prickly heat.

—Judi

Especially for You

Vanilla is wonderful as a perfume. It just happens to be one of the top five most-attractive-to-men aromas (roast turkey made the list too, but you'll probably prefer wearing vanilla).

PAMPERED PASSION PERFUME

Mix 1 drop each Vanilla, Orange, and Sandalwood. Apply the tiniest amount to your pulse points. If you like it, mix more (10 drops of each) and store it in a small dark glass bottle. You should still use the smallest amount; it lasts a long time on your skin. If you want to use it as a perfume in an atomizer, add 2 ounces of alcohol to the essential oils.

TREATING MAN'S BEST FRIEND
WITH LOVE AND AROMATHERAPY

You can also do a lot to keep your pet healthier and happier with aromatherapy. Our research for this book focused primarily on dogs. Geranium and Lavender are a favorite for dog's skin. Peppermint is a must for itches and irritation. The following two recipes will be greatly appreciated by your four-legged children when they are itchy or have dandruff.

Now, you might think I'm crazy when I tell you that the next recipe can be used on the hair of both humans and animals. Well, you may be right about my being crazy, but my dog and I are living proof that this blend works.

—Judi

PET PROTECTION

3 drops Cedar

3 drops Rosemary

2 drops Tea Tree

Mix oils together.

Add this blend to ½ ounce olive oil. Massage into scalp for 10 minutes. Leave on for 1 hour. Then wash with mild shampoo.

FLEA ATTACK

To put an extra punch into your attack against fleas, add 6 drops Tea Tree to a mild shampoo—but remember to wash your pet outside so that the fleas run for cover *outside* your home.

❧ Here we go again with a blend that is practical for use on both human and animal species.

—Judi

EARACHE REMEDY

3 drops Chamomile

1 drop Lavender

1 drop Tea Tree

Mix oils together.

↬ Put blend into 1 teaspoon of warm olive oil. For your four-legged friends, place 1 drop of the blend in each ear, and massage around the ear.

↬ For your two-legged friends (yes, it works for people, too), massage up the neck, around the ear area, and across the related cheekbone.

Warning: Take care when applying warm olive oil to ensure that the temperature of the blend is near body temperature.

Making Tea Tree Your Friend

If you are just starting out in the world of aromatherapy and want to restrict yourself to only a few oils, Tea Tree is one of the "must-have" oils, as is Lavender. The breadth of its healing properties ensures that Tea Tree is an oil you will use often.

Because many companies that produce cosmetics and hygienic products now recognize the antiseptic, antiviral, and antibacterial value of Tea Tree, it is increasingly easy to find products such as toothpaste, mouthwash, or deodorant in your health food store or grocery store that include the essential oil.

If you like Tea Tree, you might also like Naiouli, which is from the same plant family. This essential oil has a scent that is a cross between Tea Tree and Eucalyptus, which you might find milder than Tea Tree. Naiouli works well with most of the same issues as Tea Tree.

OIL OF THE MONTH

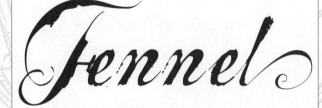

Foeniculum vulgare

They will come again, the leaf and the flower,
   to arise
From squalor of rottenness into the old
   splendour,
And magical scents to a wondering memory
   bring;
The same glory, to shine upon different eyes.
                              —*Laurence Binyon,*
                              The Burning of the Leaves

hold off on the snow for just a little longer

food, food, and more food

football

must wear a sweatshirt today

great smells wafting from the kitchen

brisk and clear but shorter days

thankful for so much

family, friends, and health

Poor November

There are a few months of the year that seem to have one major event in them that overshadows the rest of the entire month. What Valentine's Day is to February, Thanksgiving is to November.

November is a month of "too much." It starts on November 1, with too much candy from Halloween, and moves quickly into too much gray in the skies and chill in the bones. Then, of course, there is the too much of Thanksgiving feasting, coupled with too much football. And then the month closes out with too much hoopla over the next upcoming event, the official first day of the Christmas season.

The symptoms of "too much" can affect everyone in the family. From your child's overindulgence in candy, to the adults' overindulgence in holiday foods. And of course, in any month women can have "too much" PMS.

That's why you couldn't find a better oil for November than Fennel. You might be thinking, isn't fennel some kind of herb used in some breads and cookies? You're right. Isn't it also a plant that looks like celery but tastes like licorice? Right again. So why is Fennel so perfect for November?

Think of it this way: You could buy a woman's magazine for November with a svelte woman on the front cover suggesting creative ways to cook carrots and celery that will

A sound mind in a sound body is a short but full description of a happy state in the world.

—*John Locke*

satisfy your craving for the biggest piece of pumpkin pie you ever ate, or you can learn how Fennel can help you feel svelte and cute after you eat that big piece of pumpkin pie.

The choice is yours, but we're sure you'll find Fennel just right for fighting off that November feeling of too much.

Fennel

Fennel is made from the seeds of the herb. These are the same seeds used in cooking. The Fennel used for producing the essential oil is primarily grown in Mediterranean countries.

When most people think of Fennel, the essential oil, they think of it as help for digestive problems, which is its most noted attribute. Great also as a stomach tonic and antispasmodic, Fennel helps reduce flatulence and remedy abdominal cramps, even in children.

Since Fennel helps neutralize toxicity in the body, it is a great warrior against the "too much" syndrome of November. Whether you overindulge in alcohol, nicotine, food, or all of the above, Fennel might just be the oil you are looking for.

You may also be interested to know that Fennel plays a pleasant part in a woman's life. Its estrogen-stimulating properties make it useful for treating PMS by relieving menstrual pains and helping to regulate weak, irregular periods.

For new mothers, Fennel has been helpful in increasing the milk supply for our new breastfed bundles of joy.

The versatility of Fennel continues: It serves as a wonderful treatment for fighting wrinkles, dehydrated skin, and puffy, dark-shadowed eyes. It is also used in creams and body lotions to tighten and enlarge breasts. When added to face and body lotions, Fennel acts as a moisturizer.

If the hectic holiday planning and preparation makes you a bit frazzled, you'll find that Fennel calms the body and mind, which in turn reduces stress and nervousness.

Remedies

There are several ways to gain benefit from Fennel; many blends use Fennel in a massage oil. These are particularly helpful for indigestion and digestive problems that cause upper abdominal pain and flatulence.

Fennel oil can also be used to massage the breasts of mothers who are nursing to increase the production of breast milk.

A massage blend that includes Fennel is a terrific treat for your face, especially if you start off giving yourself a facial sauna.

Fennel is equally effective when mixed in water, particularly in baths to calm yourself, or as a skin tightener in a facial sauna.

What was Paradise but a Garden?
—*William Coles*

Especially for You

Spiky, spirited
Rich, deep, and inviting scent
Magic of warm isles

Clove is a delightful oil that will help ease you into the holiday season. Clove has a distinctive scent that reminds you of the holidays; it's spicy and warm and sweet. Clove is taken from the dried flower buds of an evergreen tree *(Eugenia caryophyllata)* grown in the Phillippines and the West Indies. Clove oil is a mental stimulant, an analgesic, and helps romance. Here's a way to spark up a flower arrangement in your home that will bring a smile to your lips.

SCENTED DELIGHT

Create a dried flower arrangement or buy one at the store. Put a few drops of Clove in the arrangement and place on the table.

MOMMY, MY TUMMY HURTS

One Halloween my brothers, sister, and I got grounded. Our father walked around the entire neighborhood telling all our neighbors that our mother wouldn't let us out. He came home with more candy than we could have dreamed of. We ate as much as we could before Mom caught us. Needless to say, she was up all night helping us with intense tummy-aches, never once scolding us. How she dealt with my father on this—well, let's just say the doghouse was more crowded that night.

—Judi

Sometimes it's "Honey, my stomach hurts." Every parent or spouse has heard that line several times in their life, usually late in the evening and usually following a hectic day. The day after Halloween is almost guaranteed to bring with it digestive problems for our children, who are also wired due to the caffeine and sugar in most Halloween goodies.

Let's see how Fennel can help with this indulgence. We have one recipe that is used as a massage for stomachaches. A second deals with flatulence, often a side-effect of stomachaches. We also have a suggestion to offset hiccups when your gassiness is escaping from both ends, and you are nothing more than a gaseous mass.

STOMACHACHE REMEDY

2 drops Fennel

3 drops Peppermint

Mix oils together in 1 teaspoon of vegetable oil.

Massaging the blend in a clockwise direction, massage both the lower and upper abdomen.

FLATULENCE BUSTER

10 drops Fennel

Mix all 10 drops of Fennel in 2 tablespoons of vegetable oil.

Massaging the blend in a clockwise direction, rub both the lower and upper abdomen several times a day.

Warning: *Flatulence Buster can be used safely by pregnant women as a massage. It is not recommended that pregnant women ingest Fennel or any essential oil.*

HICCUP CURE

For hiccups, put 1 drop of Fennel in a brown paper bag. Hold it over your nose and mouth and breathe deeply and slowly through your nose.

FENNEL FAVORITES FOR FEMALES

Fennel is a favorite for females because it helps us through very significant events in our lives. We all remember our first menstrual cramps and how we thought there could be no pain worse than that. Well, Fennel can help with the crampiness and by reducing the emotional impact of PMS that leaves one apathetic, tired, and listless.

'Mid pleasures and palaces
though we may roam
Be it ever so humble, there's no
place like home.
—*John Howard Payne*

◈ ◈

❧ I used to be one of those women who became a psychotic killer for several days each month. I envied my friends who were merely tired and lethargic or unapproachable unless you had a box of tissues with you. Fortunately, aromatherapy offers a safe, natural, and effective solution for all these varieties of PMS symptoms.
—Judi

PMS LETHARGY REMEDY

8 drops Chamomile

7 drops Clary Sage

7 drops Fennel

8 drops Geranium

Mix all oils together and add them to 2 tablespoons vegetable oil.

Massage in a **V** pattern up from the vaginal area, over the lower abdomen and hips, back towards the buttock and end the **V** above the anus.

KEEP USING IT

To gain the greatest benefit from this recipe, massage every day of the month, including those during which you have your period. Our research suggests that it takes between two and three months of continual use to notice a substantial effect. But just think—from then on, we don't have to lock ourselves away for a few days each month.

If you happen to be one of those not-so-lucky women who experience not only the symptoms of PMS but the ensuing menstrual cramps that are so severe that you want to stay in bed for days with a hot-water bottle, help is on the way.

MENSTRUAL CRAMP REMEDY

3 drops Chamomile

4 drops Fennel

4 drops Lavender

Mix oils together and add them to 2 tablespoons vegetable oil.

Massage the blend in a **V** pattern up from the vaginal area, over the lower abdomen and hips, back towards the buttocks, and end the **V** above the anus.

TWICE THE RELIEF

Again we have found that the greatest benefit from this recipe is received when you massage every day. While you could use both the PMS and cramp massages at the same time each day, you might want to use one massage in the morning and the other in the evening. Why not pamper yourself twice a day?

For our pregnant readers, we suggest that you do additional research about pregnancy and aromatherapy because there are several wonderful blends for each phase of pregnancy, delivery, and afterwards.

Some of these blends include essential oils that are not a part of our basic kit. So spoil yourself with some worthwhile reading and discover how aromatherapy can be a partner during this miraculous time of your life.

The following two recipes have proven to be extremely effective in dealing with increasing the production of breast milk and assisting with postnatal depression.

————————— ✺ ✺ —————————

NURSING MILK PRODUCTION RECIPE

5 drops Clary Sage

5 drops Fennel

5 drops Geranium

Mix oils together, then add the blend to 2 tablespoons of vegetable oil.

Massage the breasts once a day in a circular motion. Make sure you wipe the oils off your breasts before nursing.

————————— ✺ ✺ —————————

POSTNATAL DEPRESSION BUSTER

Fennel, Clary Sage, or Geranium

You can use any of these oils on their own or in any combination:

↠ Use 30 drops in 2 tablespoons of vegetable oil as a massage.

❦ When my friends had babies and spent weeks afterwards crying, I was terrified about becoming a mother. I never understood the phrase, "I'm so happy I could cry" until after my daughter was born.

—Judi

↬ Use 2–3 drops in a room diffuser.

↬ Use 4–6 drops in a bath.

BABY, YOU'VE GOT SOFT SKIN

Wouldn't it be wonderful if our skin could feel soft for all our years? While aromatherapy is no fountain of youth, you can bathe in many of its healing blends to help combat wrinkles and lessen the effect of puffy, shadowed eyes.

Fennel can come to the rescue. These next two recipes take just a little bit of time and yet can have such a big impact on how you feel about yourself. These blends work best for normal to oily skin.

Do you feel at times that you have too little sleep and too many things to do? On top of that, do you look like you had too little sleep and too much to do?

—Judi

FACIAL SAUNA

2 drops Fennel

2 drops Lavender

2 drops Lemon

2 drops Orange

Mix oils together and pour the blend into a bowl of steaming water.

For the greatest benefit, drape a towel over your head to contain the healing moisture.

Fennel contains hormone-like properties that encourage the firming of the skin, giving it a more youthful appearance. Fennel is used in several anti-wrinkle blends for people from age twenty to "we'll never tell." This blend seems to be particularly effective for those not-so-funny laugh lines around the eyes.

ANTI-WRINKLE REMEDY

2 drops Chamomile

2 drops Fennel

Dissolve the oils into 1 tablespoon of chilled witch hazel.

Wrap an ice cube in a soft cotton towel, dip it into the blend, and place it over your closed eyes. Leave it in place for a few seconds.

While the skin is still wet, apply a small quantity of hazel-nut oil to the area.

THE "TOO MUCH" BATTLE OF NOVEMBER

For those of you who are going to admit right here and now that you are going to overindulge during the holidays, give yourself credit for being honest with yourselves and taking responsibility for your overindulgence.

This next recipe has been found to be extremely effective for hangovers. But please make sure the designated driver gets you home safe and sound so that you can prepare this remedy.

OVERINDULGENCE RELIEVER

5 drops Fennel

3 drops Lavender

10 drops Lemon

Mix oils together.

Put 8 drops of the blend into a bath.

Rub 2 drops of the blend around the liver area and the back of the neck.

Now repeat after me: "I'll never do that again."

CAN IT BE WORSE?

Hangovers are offensive enough without adding bad breath. Mix 2 drops Fennel, 2 drops Lavender, and 2 drops Peppermint in a tumbler or warm water and gargle.

Warning: It is recommended that you only gargle with this blend, do not swallow. You should avoid ingesting most essential oils.

If the day and the night are such that you greet them with joy, and life emits a fragrance like flowers and sweet-scented herbs . . . that is your success.

—*Henry David Thoreau*

Especially for You

You can make your home smell more inviting during this holiday time by using a diffuser, potpourri pot, or the following:

COME IN OUT OF THE COLD

Keep a small pot of simmering water on the stove that includes a few drops of Clove. It is a great way to enjoy a cold winter day from inside.

More Fennel

If you like Fennel, with its strong scent reminiscent of black licorice, you might also like Anise or Cardamom essential oils, also made from seeds of the herbs.

You can find herbal teas that include these aromatic seeds in pleasant tea blends in your health food store as well as in your grocery store. You'll probably be surprised at how sweet these teas are without added sugar or honey.

Fennel seed is a wonderful ingredient in many food recipes, including chicken, fish, cheese, vegetables, rice, pasta, and dips. Many sausage blends use fennel or anise seeds, which, once you realize how these seeds can aid digestion, is a really great idea. Kind of like heading off digestive difficulties at the pass!

Happy Thanksgiving!

OIL OF THE MONTH

Orange

Citrus sinensis

If we had no Winter, the Spring would not be
so pleasant; if we did not
sometimes taste of adversity, prosperity would
not be so welcome.

—*Anne Bradstreet*

anticipation

the welcoming warm spiciness of a fireplace

sleigh rides

tree-decorating parties

sweet scent of cookies

secrets of what's to come

surprises

family plans and gatherings

Silent Night

Hectic Holidays

Surprise! It's December, and the number of shopping days left before the holiday is almost frightening now. There's so much to do. The time change (way back at the end of October) makes it seem like your day is exceedingly short. And the weekends just zoom by!

Your children astound you with their behavioral changes and their gift lists—gifts for them! Your own lists—of gifts (for others), of groceries for the festivities, and of parties and gatherings, may overwhelm you.

This is a good month to make sure you take a break for yourself. There is so much to do in such a seemingly short time. Lists, coupons, sales notices, and probably more lists are multiplying in your pocketbook. You may be getting anxious just reading this!

Let aromatherapy take you away for a while. The oil for this month is Orange, a seemingly simple enough oil. But Orange can lift a mood, smooth an anxious brow, calm and warm you—just what you need in the month of December.

Orange

The orange actually gives us several clues about Orange oil: The warm and cheery color of orange, its familiarity (made from the peel of oranges, there's nothing exotic about this essential oil), and the basic playfulness of its ball shape.

The scent of Orange seems to carry some of the smell of summer and sunshine that were needed to ripen it—perfect for December's cold weather.

Orange oil was not used medically until the seventeenth century, rather late in the history of aromatherapy. Legend has it that oranges were probably the "golden apples" of mythological times.

The sweet, warm fragrance of Orange oil is ideal for children and for adults who have forgotten their inner child and are too serious and tense.

Warning: Don't use Orange essential oil undiluted on your skin because it can irritate. Don't use Orange essential oil on your skin prior to sunbathing.

Remedies

In this chapter, you can find Orange-scented remedies for low energy, skin that is not as relaxed as it could be, and the not-surprising sleeplessness of the holiday season. You'll also discover some aromatic ways to use Orange to change air that is not as nice or fresh as it could be.

You might think, as our children do, that Orange smells just like a lollipop. This is probably why it is such a comforting oil—it smells like childhood. Orange is one of the oils that is perfect for children; it's gentle and familiar.

You can also use Orange in water-based sprays, as you will see in the recipes in this chapter.

Especially for You

Incense offering
Valued as gold by ancients
Anointing, soothing, special

Frankincense was one of the gifts of the three kings that first Christmas, along with gold and myrrh. It comes from the wood of the Boswellia thurifera, a tree of the Balm family that is found in Africa and Arabia. In ancient times, the Egyptians and Babylonians used Frankincense as sacred offerings.

Frankincense, which is also called olibanum, has a woody, incense-like scent. With its slightly Christmasy scent it reduces stress and tension—perfect for this season, don't you think? It is also a spiritual oil, helpful prior to meditating—another interesting thought for this season.

Pamper yourself by taking some time to apply the following oil to your face. Then sit, close your eyes, and relax for fifteen minutes—no cheating!

REJUVENATING OIL

Mix 8 drops Lavender, 8 drops Fennel, and 5 drops Frankincense into 2 ounces sweet almond oil or olive oil. Apply one teaspoon of this to your cleansed face. Allow time for this to be absorbed by your skin.

A few drops of Orange in a bowl of water on your gas or wood stove helps moisturize the air in your home nicely. Add a sprinkle of cinnamon for a really festive aroma. But be prepared; your family will want to know what you've been baking.

ENERGIZE ME

Who's ever got enough energy? Especially during this season? Eat right, rest (when you can), and use the following Energizer Blend in an air spray.

Lemon and Orange work well together, both supplying energy. The following spray takes advantage of this partnership:

------------------------------ ⚘ ⚘ ------------------------------

ENERGIZER BLEND

4 drops Lavender

1 drop Lemon

3 drops Orange

2 drops Rosemary

Mix the oils together and use them in one of the following ways:

🌿 The smell rejoiceth the heart of man, for which cause they used to strew [herbs and flowers] in chambers and places of recreation, pleasure, and repose, where feasts and banquets are made.

—*John Gerard*

☙ My college student son finds this blend helpful in an air spray when he's got studying to do. My secret thought is that Energizer Blend spray probably gets rid of some of that boys' locker room smell in his dorm. Now, that's got to be distracting!

—Paula

↬ Mix oils into 3 cups water and spray your work environment.

↬ Mix the above oils into 2 tablespoons canola oil for an after-bath oil in the morning. Rub the oil onto still-moist skin to seal in moisture and energize your day.

SWEET AIR

Holidays are a great time to sweeten the air with aromatic sprays. And water-based sprays are great to use in your house, especially with central heating systems that really dry out circulating air. Just be careful where you spray so no water droplets fall on wooden furniture; water can mark your wood.

Cedar and Orange are two essential oils that will bring a Christmas smell into your home. Try the following spray:

WELCOME SPRAY

4 drops Cedar

2 drops Fennel

2 drops Lemon

2 drops Orange

4 drops vanilla extract

Mix oils together and use in one of the following ways:

- Mix the blend into 2 cups water and use as an air spray.

- Mix the blend into 2 cups water and simmer on your stove or your woodstove. As the scented water slowly evaporates into the air, it humidifies as well as scents.

_____

People will wonder what you've been cooking, since your house seems so welcoming. The vanilla extract is a simple, inexpensive way to add another element to essential oils.

— ✤ ✤ —

CLOVE ORANGE

Orange (the fruit)

Alum (available from the pharmacy or grocery store)

Whole cloves from the grocery store

Stab the orange full of cloves. Shake it in a bag of the alum to coat it. Dry it out in a low oven, over a pilot light, or over a heat register.

_____

SMOKERS' AID

The following air spray is particularly effective against the smell of smoking. The nature of essential oils is that they change things, not cover them up. So the essential oils in an

When I was a Girl Scout, we made clove oranges and apples to hang in a closet or fill a bowl (much like potpourri), or to hang on the tree. Here's how to make a clove orange.

—Paula

air spray combine with and change air particles. You end up with a fresher environment than if you used most commercial ozone-destroying air deodorizing sprays.

You can also use it to clean and deodorize the air after cooking events: spills on the burner, greasy odors in the air, or fish.

The No Smokers Air Spray will not only clean the air, but provide a festive, uplifting aroma, perfect for company.

NO SMOKERS AIR SPRAY

8 drops Cedar

4 drops Lavender

5 drops Lemon

5 drops Orange

6 drops Tea Tree

Mix the above oils into 16 ounces of water and use as an air spray.

GIFT-GIVING

Scented fire-starter cones are nice gifts for friends who are fortunate enough to have fireplaces.

FIRE-STARTER CONES

Pine cones

Candle wax

Orange oil

Cedar oil

Melt the wax in a double boiler. Remove from the burner. Allow the wax to cool, but keep it liquid. Mix several drops of the Orange and Cedar oils to the slightly cooled wax mixture. Dip the cones into the cooled wax mixture. Set aside on newspaper to drip and dry.

You can also sprinkle evergreen needles on the cones before the wax dries. This gives a nice pine smell as it burns.

Use one of these Fire-Starter Cones with the kindling wood for an aromatic start to your fire.

TAKE A BREAK

You need a break when things get so busy and over-scheduled that you find yourself, Grinch-like, wishing that the holiday season was over. Personal pampering is a perfect solution to feeling overwhelmed. A slow bath with several of the more calming oils will probably give you the time and

peace to go out and face that holiday season again. Try the Relaxing Bath below. This is great at the end of a hectic day.

———————— ✃ ✄ ————————

RELAXING BATH BLEND

3 drops Chamomile

2 drops Geranium

3 drops Lavender

2 drops Orange

Mix the oils into 2 ounces hazelnut oil. Use 1 teaspoon of this bath oil in the bath.

WHEN YOUR SKIN NEEDS A BREAK

You know perfectly well (and we understand) that a lot of the time you won't be able to fit in a bath for your little pampering escape. Other touches of Orange around your home will give you some of the same feeling.

Try the following toner for oily skin.

———————— ✃ ✄ ————————

OILY SKIN TONER

3 drops Geranium

5 drops Lavender

❧ On our skin, as on a screen, the gamut of life's experiences is projected: emotions surge, sorrows penetrate, and beauty finds its depth.

—*A. Montagu*

5 drops Orange

1 tablespoon witch hazel

Mix the above ingredients. Add enough springwater to make 8 ounces. Use this as a splash on your face after cleansing and before moisturizing.

FOR SWEET DREAMS

Sleep—its restoring properties are so precious, and sometimes, when you need it the most, it is most elusive. There are several aromatic solutions to holiday-caused insomnia. Both of the following sprays are also gentle enough for your little ones.

Orange oil is cheering and familiar. This makes it work well for children. One of the best uses for children is in a bedtime spray. The following blend is a relaxing bedtime spray for children, especially for Christmas Eve, when it is *soooo* hard to fall asleep.

HOLIDAY HELPER

4 drops Cedar

2 drops Chamomile

2 drops Geranium

2 drops Orange

I put together an Orange and Lavender water spray for one of our friends' children. Talk about conditioning—eventually just peeling an orange near this very active three-year-old would cause him to yawn.

—Paula

Add the above essential oils to 3 cups water. Spray the bedroom just before bedtime.

Adults might like something a little different. The following blend is quick and easy and smells great.

GOOD NIGHT, IRENE REMEDY

1 drop Lavender

1 drop Orange

Put the two drops of essential oils on a handkerchief or cotton ball. Place this between your pillow and pillowcase so your head warms it all night.

That recipe is so easy it's like cheating, but try it. Its lovely, old-fashioned smell will lull you to sleep.

For More Zing in Your Life

Enjoy your holidays. Use Orange with its sweet, warm fragrance to stay attuned to what is really important about this season—your family and loved ones, hospitality, and a sense of welcome.

If you like Orange, and who wouldn't, you might also like Bergamot, Mandarin, Tangerine, or Neroli. Bergamot,

Mandarin, and Tangerine are made from the peels of their associated fruits; their scents vary slightly from the scent of Orange. Neroli is made from orange blossoms. It's a sweet, flowery, expensive oil that is used in many perfumes.

For a very comforting afternoon break, try some orange spice tea. Your grocery store has many brands and combinations to choose from. You can get a spiced orange with real tea or an orange-scented herbal blend. Perfect for a quick, warming break in your hectic afternoon.

Use dried orange peels in potpourri. You can buy these ready-made, or find a recipe in a craft book to make your own. Make extra for gifts! This potpourri is good either dry or simmering in a pot.

HOLIDAY POTPOURRI

For a simple, easy-to-make potpourri, use a vegetable peeler to peel the orange zest from several oranges (or grapefruits), enough to make a cup of zest. Dry these strips of zest. Add 4 cinnamon sticks or 2 tablespoons powdered cinnamon. Use about a quarter-cup of this mix to 2 cups of water for simmering.

Nothing awakens a reminiscence like an odor.

—*Victor Hugo*

Once you get started, you'll probably find lots of ways to make use of the familiar, comforting aroma of Orange. And relax. It's time for a new year.

Especially for You

Take some time to relax and remember what the season is all about. Try the following combination on a lamp ring. Use this to scent the room in which you meditate or practice yoga.

MEDITATION MIX

Apply one drop each of Sandalwood, Cedar, and Frankincense directly to a lamp ring. Sit and relax.

Aromatically Yours

Aren't essential oils terrific? As you journeyed with us through the months of this year, you've learned about twelve of the most useful aromatherapy oils and twelve exotic and fun oils. You've also learned how to incorporate aromatherapy into your life, into your home, and into your family. You've probably never felt like you were casting a spell, not even once—except maybe that one time last July with those pesky mosquitoes. We hope that you've been trying your own blends—you're certainly ready to.

We couldn't let you go without sharing some parting thoughts. See if you agree with our feelings and impressions:

WHEN YOU USE...	DON'T YOU FEEL...?
Cedar	Earthy, calm, like running in the woods with the wind blowing in your healthy hair.
Chamomile	Settled, childlike, like snuggling up with a blanket and a cup of tea.
Clary Sage	Mellow, relaxed, like melting in a warm bath with candles and a soft music.
Eucalyptus	Healthy, cleansed, like taking deep breaths of clean, fresh air.
Fennel	Content, satisfied, like taking a long walk after a large gourmet meal.

Geranium	Sweet, sensuous, like braiding flowers into your hair and running barefoot in a meadow.
Lavender	Fresh, happy, like sitting quietly watching a beautiful sunrise.
Lemon	Exhilarated, bright, like tackling the biggest task that lies ahead of you with the solid knowledge that you will succeed.
Orange	Juicy, fruity, like playing with children full of laughter and getting sticky.
Peppermint	Brisk, vibrant, like grabbing ski poles and daring that slope.
Rosemary	Stimulated, pampered, like spraying it all over your stuffy workplace.
Tea Tree	Healed, germ-free, like you're armed to face any germ warfare.

↢ ↢ ↢

Thank you for sharing our journey into the world of aromatherapy. We hope you enjoy using this book as much as we enjoyed writing it.

Wishing you health, beauty, and happiness in your life, we are essentially yours,

Judi & Paula

❦ The human body is the best picture of the human soul.
—*Wittgenstein*

RESOURCE GUIDE

❧ Amphora
5513 6th Avenue South
Seattle, WA 98108
(206) 762-1354
Nine store locations throughout the U.S.
Please call for more information.

❧ Aphrodisia
164 Bleeker Street
New York, NY 10014
(212) 989-6440
Store and mail order for over 200 essential oils.
Call for list.

❧ Aromatic Plant Project & Jeanne Rose
    Aromatherapy
219 Carl Street
San Francisco, CA 94117
(415) 564-6785

Catalog of aromatherapy education books and authentic
hydrosols and aromatherapy kits.

❧ Aroma Vera Inc.
P. O. Box 3609
Culver City, CA 90231
(310) 280-0407
Stores and catalog for essential oils. Call for locations.

❧ As We Change
6335 Ferris Square, Suite A
San Diego, CA 92121
800-203-5585

Catalog for women over forty; includes essential oils,
scented candles.

❧ Aura Cacia
Weaverville, CA 96093
www.frontierherb.com

❧ Avon Products Inc.
1345 6th Avenue
New York, NY 10105
(212) 282-7000

Please call for more information.

❧ Bed, Bath & Beyond
650 Liberty Avenue
Union, NJ 07083
(908) 688-0888

Over 150 stores throughout the U.S. Please call for more information.

❧ The Body Shop by Mail
45 Horsehill Road
Hanover Technical Center
Cedar Knolls, NJ 07927
800-541-2535

Essential oils and aromatherapy products.

❧ Bare Escentuals
1300 Industrial Road, Ste. 14
San Carlos, CA 94070
800-227-3990

Stores featuring aromatherapy products, essential oils. Call for locations.

❧ Body Time
1341 Seventh Street
Berkeley, CA 94710
(510) 524-0360

Stores and catalog featuring aromatherapy products, essential oils. Call for locations or to be put on mailing list.

❧ Capriland's Herb Farm
Silver Street
North Coventry, CT 06238
(203) 742-7244

Essential oils.

❧ Caswell-Massey Co. Ltd.
Catalogue Division
P.O. Box 7015
100 Enterprise Place
Dover, DE 19904-8208
800-326-0500

Soaps, perfumes, lotions, and other miscellaneous bath products.

❧ Chambers
3250 Van Ness Avenue
San Francisco, CA 94109
(415) 421-7900

Aromatherapy products. Please call for more information.

❧ Common Scents Catalog
3920 24th Street
San Francisco, CA 94114
(415) 826-1019

Essential oils.

⊹ Cost Plus
201 Clay Street
Oakland, CA 94607
(510) 893-7300
*Seventy-three stores throughout the U.S featuring
aromatherapy products. Please call for locations.*

⊹ Costco
800 Lake Drive
Issaquah, WA 98027
800-220-6000
*Over 280 warehouses thoughout the U.S. Please call for
locations.*

⊹ Crabtree and Evelyn Catalog
Mail Order Division
P. O. Box 158
Woodstock, CT 06281
800-272-2873
Bath and skin care products, essential oils.

⊹ Crate & Barrel
725 Landwer Road
Northbrook, IL 60062
(847) 272-2888
*Seventy-five stores throughout the U.S. Please call for
more information.*

⊹ Earthsake
1817 Second Street
Berkeley, CA 94710
(510) 848-5023

*Several stores in the San Francisco Bay Area; aromat-
herapy products and essential oils. Call for locations.*

⊹ Energy Essentials
P. O. Box 470785
San Francisco, CA 94147
(415) 753-3382
Essential oils.

⊹ Essentially Yours
P. O. Box 81865
Bakersfield, CA 93380
*Mail order service for essential oils. Send a SASE for
catalog.*

⊹ Femail Creations
(702) 270-9153
Aromatherapy products.

⊹ Frontier Cooperative Herbs
Box 299
Norway, IA 52318
800-669-3275
www.frontierherb.com
Essential oils.

⊹ Gaia Products
62 Kent Street
Brooklyn, NY 11222
(718) 389-8224
Essential oils.

⊸ Gardener's Eden
800-822-9600

Aromatherapy products.

⊸ Green Mountain Herbs Ltd.
P. O. Box 2369
Boulder, CO 80306
800-525-2696

Essential oils.

⊸ Green World Mercantile
2340 Polk St.
San Francisco, CA 94109
(415) 771-5717

Aromatherapy bar, classes, and huge selection of essential oils.

⊸ Hausmann's Pharmacy, Inc.
534-536 W. Girard Avenue
Philadelphia, PA 19123
800-235-5522

Essential oils.

⊸ Headlines
838 Market Street, Suite 400
San Francisco, CA 94102
(415) 989-8240, ext. 0

Six stores throughout the U.S featuring aromatherapy products. Please call for locations.

⊸ HealthyHome
960C Harvest Drive

Blue Bell, PA 19422
800-988-1127

Aromatherapy products.

⊸ Hearthsong
170 Professional Center Dr.
Rohnert Park, CA 94928
800-432-6314

Aromatherapy products for adults and children. Catalog and stores; call for locations or to be put on mailing list.

⊸ Hove Parfumeur Ltd. Catalog
824 Royal Street
New Orleans, LA 70116
(504) 525-7827

Essential oils.

⊸ Kiehl's Pharmacy
109 Third Avenue
New York, NY 10003
(212) 475-3400

Store featuring essential oils.

⊸ Liberty Natural Products, Inc.
8120 SE Stark Street
Portland, OR 97215-2346
800-289-8427
Fax: (503) 256-1182
E-mail: liberty@teleport.com
www.libertynatural.com

Importer-distributor of botanicals and supplier of ingredients for recipes in Seasons of Aromatherapy.

⊕ Natural Apothecary of Vermont
170 Whitney Hill Road
Brookline, VT 05345
(802) 365–7156
Fax: (802) 365–4029
E-mail: matpag@sover.net

⊕ Natural Wellness
80 Golden Boulevard
Walden, NY 12586
(914) 744-5027
Aromatherapy products.

⊕ Natural Wonders
4209 Technology Drive
Fremont, CA 94538
(510) 252-9600
Over 175 stores throughout the U.S featuring aromatherapy products. Please call for locations.

⊕ Nature's Herb
1010 46th Street
Emeryville, CA 94608
(510) 601-0700
Essential oils.

⊕ Nordstroms
1321 Second Ave.
Seattle, WA 98101
800-723-2889
Nationwide chain featuring aromatherapy products. Please call for locations.

⊕ Original Swiss Aromatics
Pacific Institute of Aromatherapy
P. O. Box 6842
San Rafael, CA 94903
(415) 459-3998
Aromatherapy supplies, essential oils.

⊕ Pier 1 Imports
301 Commerce Street, Suite 600
Fort Worth, TX 76102
(817) 878-8000
Seven hundred and fifty stores throughout the U.S featuring aromatherapy products. Please call for locations.

⊕ Potpourri Collection Catalog
120 North Meadows Road
Medfield, MA 02052
(508) 359-7702
Aromatherapy products.

⊕ Real Good Trading
555 Leslie Street
Ukiah, CA 95482
(707) 468-9292
Catalog and stores throughout the country. Please call for locations or to be put on mailing list.

⊕ Red Rose
800-374-5505
Aromatherapy products in catalog and stores; call for locations or to be put on mailing list.

∾ Self Care Catalog
5850 Shellmound Street
Emeryville, CA 94608
800-345-3371

Aromatherapy products.

∾ The Sharper Image Spa
800-344-4444

Aromatherapy products.

∾ Simmons Handcrafts
42295 Highway 36
Bridgeville, CA 95526
800-428-0412

Natural products for home and personal care.

∾ Smith & Hawken
117 E. Strawberry Drive
Mill Valley, CA 94941
(415) 383-4415

*Catalog and thirty stores throughout the U.S featuring
aromatherapy products. Please call for locations or to be
put on mailing list.*

∾ Urban Outfitters
1809 Walnut Avenue
Philadelphia, PA 19103
(215) 564-2313

*Over thirty stores throughout the U.S. Please call for
locations.*

∾ Well & Good Catalog
1000 Westgate Drive
St. Paul, MI 55114
(612) 659-3700

Aromatherapy products.

∾ Whole Life Products
1334 Pacific Avenue
Forest Grove, OR 97116
800-634-9057

Aromatherapy products, essential oils.

∾ Wild Oats Markets
1645 Broadway
Boulder, CO 80302
(303) 440-5220

*Fifty-eight stores throughout the U.S featuring aro-
matherapy products. Please call for locations.*

∾ Wild Women Enterprises
P.O. Box 114
North Brighton, MA 02764
(508) 880-0555

Aromatherapy products.

∾ Yves Rocher Inc.
P. O. Box 158
Champlain, NY 12919
800-321-4909

Aromatherapy products.

ACKNOWLEDGMENTS

We are indebted to a number of people who allowed us to experiment on them, who allowed us to grill them for thoughts and reactions to our ever-changing blends, and who read our recipes and text and gave their opinions freely. We would like to thank, in alphabetical order: Katherine Bates, Lynne Bennett, Tim Bennett, Nancy Cobb, Karen Cwikla, Marie Fitzsimmons, Brian Gadoury, Connie Gagnon, Chelsea Gunn, Jillian Hughes, William Hughes, Mark Hyjek, Cathy Murphy, Debbie Neal, Mary Page, Margaret Provost, Ellen Simes, and Becca Torns.

ABOUT THE AUTHORS

Judith Fitzsimmons is a certified aromatherapist living in Tennessee. Paula M. Bousquet, who lives and gardens organically on a horse farm in Georgia, has been involved with aromatherapy and herb gardening since 1992. You can reach Paula at www.synergygroup.com/sites/greenwold.

INDEX

CONARI PRESS, established in 1987, publishes books on topics ranging from psychology, spirituality, and women's history to sexuality, parenting, and personal growth. Our main goal is to publish quality books that will make a difference in people's lives—both how we feel about ourselves and how we relate to one another.

Our readers are our most important resource, and we value your input, suggestions, and ideas. We'd love to hear from you—after all, we are publishing books for you!

To request our latest book catalog, or to be added to our mailing list, please contact:

CONARI PRESS

2550 Ninth Street, Suite 101
Berkeley, California 94710-2551
800-685-9595 • fax: 510-649-7190
e-mail: Conaripub@aol.com
Website: http://www.readersNdex.com/conari/